FORGET ME NOT

J.M. MADDEN

Forget Me Not

by J.M. Madden

ACKNOWLEDGMENTS

As always I have to thank my family. I love you guys dearly and thank you for putting up with my craziness.

Sandie, you are such an incredible sounding board and friend. Mayas, you always give it to me straight. Thank you girls! JoAnn, thank you so much for the medical input. All three of you helped me so much.
Thank you!

Meg (aka. Wonder Woman) You rock! Thank you for all the work you did shaping me up! And those damn timelines…

Author Note

This book had a strange feel to it. It felt almost … precognitive. Or something. That's not exactly the word I need. There was some strange mojo going on.

My computer was acting hinky, when it never has before. There were things that I wrote into the book that started happening around me. A friend of mine fell and broke her upper arm- like one of the characters in the book. Another friend's husband had a heart attack- like one of the characters in the book.

I was worried about doing anything else to any more of the characters. Truly!

But I did write in a scene about a ranch hand winning the lottery.

If any of you readers win money, I expect a 50% split!!! Just kidding … kinda…

Readers, be sure to read all the way to the end! There's a chapter of Brock's book, Untying His Not!

This is for Karen and Kenny. Hopefully Chad and Lora can have 25 years like you guys did! Much love!

CHAPTER 1

DUNCAN FROWNED UP AT CHAD. "This is kind of getting to be a habit," he murmured.

Chad winced. "I know. Something came up in New York and Lora had to wait for a conference call. If we had known ahead of time, we could have gotten Heather to pick Mercy up at school, but she's doing something else."

Duncan rubbed his jaw and nodded. "Go get her and bring her in, then. I'll watch the live feed while you do."

Chad felt even more guilty. Damn, he hadn't realized Duncan was the only one in the office to do this. "Roger's not available?"

With a crooked grin, Duncan shook his head. "You know he's cut his hours since he and Cass got together at Christmas."

Yeah, he had known that. Things had changed in the past several months. All good changes, of course, but different none-the-less. Their schedules had had to be more fluid than ever with employees and friends coming and going.

"I'll be back as soon as I can," he promised. "Literally, nothing has happened in the time the feed has been live."

"I'll be fine, Chad. Go get your girl."

Without another word he headed out of the office. The surprise spring snow from last night had mostly been burned away by the sunlight, and the temperature was rising, so there shouldn't be any delays in getting back.

Duncan was a good guy. Too damn good sometimes. There weren't many men that would cover for his guys the way Duncan did. Maybe it would be a good time to mention to boss man that they needed to hire more veterans. Chad knew for a fact Duncan still had a stack of resumés in his bottom drawer.

Chad drove to the school a few miles away, getting there as the last of the buses left. As they pulled away, he could see a couple of kids sitting on the broad front steps of the school, as well as Mercy's second grade teacher. There was a scowl on her pretty, young face, and he didn't blame her. He parked the truck at the curb and smiled in spite of the disapproval in her expression.

"Hello, Ms. Clark. I know I missed parent pick-up. Plans changed at the last minute and I had to scramble."

She sighed as she opened the door for Mercy to climb in. "That's fine, Mr. Lowell, we just like to have prior notice when your child has to be pulled off the bus."

He winced and glanced at Mercy. She didn't seem any the worse for wear, but he was learning that she didn't always show the world everything going on in her heart. "Yes, ma'am. I understand."

Determined to be charming, Chad gave her a smile and she seemed to soften. "Well, okay then. Bye, Mercy. I'll see you tomorrow."

"Bye, Ms. Clark."

Mercy climbed into her booster seat in the back and Chad circled the truck to fasten her in. When she wouldn't look at him, he paused. "You okay, darlin'?

She nodded her head, glancing up. "Mom forgot, huh?"

His heart ached at the resignation he could see in her big green eyes.

"No, she didn't forget. She had a big conference call with New York she had to take."

Mercy turned to look out the opposite window and Chad knew it didn't matter what he said. Her mother wasn't here in this moment. That was what mattered.

With a kiss to her forehead he tucked some of the hair that had fallen from her ponytail behind her ear. He shut the door and circled back around. He prodded her several times with conversation, but she was pretty bull-headed. She gave him short answers, but didn't expand on anything. The only time her expression brightened was when she realized they were heading to the Lost And Found offices. "Is Duncan there?"

Chad nodded, grinning. "Yup, he is. Maybe I should have sent him to pick you up?"

She nodded. "I'd like that."

When they headed into the offices, she grinned up at Duncan like they were old friends, which, Chad supposed, they were. Though the boss man was not used to kids, they seemed to love him. Maybe *because* he wasn't used to them. Duncan talked to them like they were adults.

"Hello, Miss Mercy. Where's your hat? It's still pretty chilly out."

Mercy pulled the hat from her backpack and brandished it at him. "It's getting warm out now, though. Almost all the snow is gone."

Duncan cocked a brow at her. "I guess you're right. I need you to come with me. Somebody erased the picture you drew me on the whiteboard. Do you believe that? I need a new one."

They wandered off toward Duncan's office, Mercy skipping with excitement.

When they headed home a few hours later, Chad worried that she would get discouraged again, but Lora was there at the door waiting for them. Mercy whooped and ran into her mother's arms as soon as Chad set her down from the truck. Lora stroked her hair and asked her where her hat was. Rather than answer her, Mercy told her that Duncan had asked her the same thing.

Chad took his time getting to the door, aware that he had a bit of resentment rattling around inside him. Actually, he had a couple of bits of resentment.

When Lora looked up at him, though, her expression clear of everything but love, it was hard to stay aggravated at her. "Hello, darlin'."

Dropping a kiss to her lips, he wrapped an arm around her, bumping her inside so that he could close the door behind them. Lora moaned into his mouth and ran a hand into his hair. "I needed this."

He did too, he realized. It had been a couple of days since they'd really connected. More than that since they'd actually made love.

"I did too, babe."

She pulled away a little too quickly, but excitement shone in her eyes. "You should have seen the meeting I just ran. It was incredible. There were CEOs from several major east coast banks, and I talked to them like I knew what I was saying."

Chad laughed, loving the look of confidence in her luminous green eyes. "That sounds daunting."

"It was at first," she admitted, "but they want to do business with our company, so they were kind of kissing my ass."

"Was William there?"

The middle-aged executive had been hired to operate the

investment company day to day, and he'd been teaching Lora as much as possible via conference calls. It wasn't the most ideal way to do it, being on opposite ends of the country, but it seemed to be working for them. Chad had gone to bed the past few nights long before Lora had. As he'd walked down the hallway to their room, he'd heard the soft tones of her voice through the office door, talking money things he had no earthly idea about.

He would say that for Lora. After Derek had gone off the deep end and come after them, Lora had stopped him in the most definitive way possible. She'd taken his life to protect her daughter in the attempted kidnapping. She'd saved her own life, too; Derek would have killed her without a second thought. After that, the company had been given to Lora to hold in trust for Mercy. Rather than completely giving the operating over to a nameless face who didn't care about fostering a heritage, she'd started taking classes and learning the business for herself. She had the determination of a bull.

When she wasn't learning from William Styles Jr., the proxy they'd hired to run the company, she was at the local community college taking business classes, absorbing as much information as she possibly could as quickly as she could. The once a week class had now transitioned into three times a week online, several hours at a time.

In his heart Chad knew that she was trying to secure her daughter's future, but he hated the time that it was taking away from them.

"I didn't have time to get anything for dinner, so I thought we'd order out."

He sighed, nodding. That's what he'd expected. Maybe he needed to take over the kitchen. Mercy loved his French toast.

The new house they'd moved into was in a very good location for takeout. Besides the standard pizza and oriental food, they also had a Thai and a Mexican place they ordered from regularly. Tonight they settled on that. As Mercy crunched through tortilla chips she chattered about her day. Chad was feeling quiet, so he just let her talk.

"Is something wrong?"

Lora's eyes were concerned as she rested a hand on his knee.

"I'm fine."

He wouldn't say anything about his concerns in front of Mercy. He could do that later.

But later never came. By the time he cleaned up the rest of the takeout, Lora was making sure Mercy did everything she was supposed to do before bed. Chad missed their nightly rituals of reading two books before bed. She was getting a little old for that now. Maybe it was time to start a couple chapters at a time of longer books, like Harry Potter or something like that. Hmmm, was Louis L'Amour too grown up to read to a kid? He'd started reading them when he was about nine or ten. While he was thinking it over, he went in to kiss her goodnight and chat just a few minutes. While he was chatting, Lora disappeared with an armload of laundry. Chad didn't see her again until she was heading into her office. When he ducked his head around the door jamb, she had put her headphones on to listen to a class.

Damn it.

Things were going to have to change soon.

CHAPTER 2

LORA FELT like her brain was going to explode. All of the words were running together and beginning to confuse her. She was supposed to get to the end of this chapter before class tomorrow, but she didn't think it was going to happen. Widening her eyes to force alertness, she reached out for a swallow of tea, but it was long gone cold.

Sighing, she pulled the headphones from her ears. There was an immediate loosening in her skull, like they had been on too tight and she just hadn't noticed. Ouch...

She glanced out the window to get an idea of time, but the security lights were obscured by fog. There was no way to tell what time it was. Heading for the door she listened for movement in the house, but there was no chance of this. This new house was the most secure she'd ever been in, with tile floors and nice thick walls. Safe, secure. But pretty much soundproof.

The kitchen was dark and all of the food had been put away. Chad, obviously. Her heart warmed at the thought of him. He had been such a huge help recently.

Lora felt like she was a kid again, going to school and

learning. Though she'd never had any leanings toward banks or money, it was becoming second nature to her. When she and Derek had been married, she'd been beyond frustrated by the lack of control in her marriage. As a woman and as a mother, she'd had no say in anything. She'd been subjugated and humiliated and it had taken an extreme act of courage to break away from the Malone money. Rosalind, her former mother-in-law, even as cold and unsupportive as she'd been, had been a mother figure to her and given guidance to Lora after Mercy was born.

Lora paused as she circled the marble island, coming to a slow halt. *Had* Rosalind actually been a mother figure to her? No, not really. Lora's own mother Mary had died a year before she'd met Derek and her life had gone to hell. Mary had been a real mother, loving and encouraging, until ovarian cancer had taken her down.

Every bit of her own mothering instincts she attributed to her own mother. She wouldn't credit Rosalind with anything, other than creating the monster that had ruined all their lives.

It made her sad that her mother had never met her grand-daughter, and vise versa. Mary had been an incredible woman.

And Francine Lowell was an incredible mother. It had taken her a while to warm up to Chad's mother, but now that she had she couldn't imagine her not being in their lives. It had been a few days since she'd talked to them...

Pulling her phone from her pocket, she scrolled to the calendar. It had been months, Christmas time, since they'd actually *seen* the Lowells. She should talk to talk to Chad about going for a visit.

She laughed. Like she had a lot of spare time for visiting.

Tiredness dragged at her mind. She needed to go to bed

and recharge. Turning off all the lights but the one above the sink, she left the kitchen and headed to bed.

Chad didn't move when she climbed between the sheets, but she curled against his broad back, tucking her hands against her chest. The feel of his hot, smooth skin against her own made her wish he was awake. It would be nice to cuddle for a while.

These damn classes were really getting in the way of living life, but she had to keep at them. She knew in the long run it would be the best thing to secure Mercy's future.

CHAD WOKE EARLY, stretching hard. He also had the boner from hell. He peeked across the expanse of the bed, hoping to see his fiancée, but Lora was already gone. She'd been there in the night, he remembered the feel of her hand on his waist and stroking his back, but he hadn't woken enough to talk to her. And now she was gone again. It was Friday, so she had an early class. He probably wouldn't see her until tonight.

And he needed to get Mercy to school. Grabbing his phone from the bedside table, he peered at the screen. Fuck... he was already ten minutes late. He must have snoozed it without realizing it.

Moving to the side of the bed, he reached for his sleeve and prosthetic. There was a wear spot building on the outside of the stump. He needed to make time to take the thing in and get refitted.

He'd have to add it to the never-ending list.

"Mercy, you gotta get up baby doll," he called. "We're running late."

From down the hallway he heard a faint 'okay'... He'd have to hurry through his shower and go wake her again in five minutes. Hopefully Lora had laid out her clothes the night before like she normally did.

The entire morning was a manic rush, but they managed to get to school a few minutes before the final bell rang. One of the school monitors watched Mercy as she ran into the school, and Chad cringed. The outfit he'd allowed the eight year old to pick out had been ... unusual, but it had been what she'd wanted. It would have taken too much time to argue for acceptable normal, so he let her go.

When he got to work he could finally relax. The thought left him chuckling and John looked at him curiously. They were back watching a live feed, waiting for a suspect to appear exactly where he wasn't supposed to. They had civil papers to serve on him and he'd been harder than an ornery mustang to catch.

"What are you laughing at?"

Chad shook his head. "Lora's been running like crazy and taking classes, getting ready to take over Malone. I've been doing everything recently, and things are falling through the cracks."

John laughed, sitting back in his wheelchair. "Oh, puhleese... you ought to try living with a pregnant female on the verge of giving birth to two babies. And a partially damn housetrained puppy. You talk about craziness?"

Chad noted that Gunny glanced over his shoulder to make sure he wasn't over heard by his fiancée. Shannon, their office manager, must be in the outer office. Chad hadn't seen her when he'd come in, but he'd been distracted.

"I have no sympathy with you and the dog, Gunny. That was your own fault for springing it on her at Christmas."

John tossed him a rare grin. "Yeah, I know, but Shannon fucking loves that dog. And the dog loves her. So it's all good in the end. At least the potty training is pretty much over with. Although she left me a present the other morning I didn't see until I'd run through it with my chair and circled the room. It took me forever to get the shit out of my tires."

Gunny leaned over to look at the side of his wheelchair and Chad laughed out loud. That was too damn funny.

Duncan walked in and parked himself behind them, arms folded and stance strong. Chad still couldn't get over how good he was doing after the hip replacement. "What's so funny?"

"Dogshit in tires," Chad told him.

Their partner barked out a laugh. "Yeah, I heard about that. Poor baby."

John flipped Duncan the bird and they all chuckled.

"No movement at all on the Watt-tech case?" Duncan asked eventually, nodding his head at the monitor.

"No. The regular employees have come through the door, but not the ex-boyfriend."

"Well, the woman called to let us know that she's had two hang-up calls this morning, making her think he's checking to make sure she'll be there. Chad, why don't you go ahead and grab the packet and head out. I have a feeling it'll be sooner rather than later when we see our friend."

Chad tipped his imaginary hat and pushed to his feet. "Will do, mon Capítane."

Duncan just shook his head at his silliness. "When did I get shuffled off to the officers' club? John will call you when he has eyes on the target."

"Gotcha."

Chad grabbed his cowboy hat and jacket from the tree by the door and left the office. Outside, the sun shone brightly on the cold, cloudless morning. Denver was well known for its amazing scenery, but Chad thought even the average blue-sky days were beautiful.

It was shocking to realize how quickly the days were going though. Every single one of the people that worked at

Lost and Found had full lives, and it seemed like this year had brought huge changes for everyone. John and Shannon were expecting two babies in early summer. Duncan had surprised them all the other day during the weekly staff meeting when he admitted that he and Alex had eloped and gotten married. That had been a shock to Chad. He'd had no idea they'd been *that* involved.

But then, Duncan always held his cards close to the vest, especially when it came to his personal life. Even the romance between Duncan and Alex had come as a surprise. Yeah, they'd all flown her out here at Christmas time to meet up with him, but he didn't think any of them expected Duncan to actually make a serious relationship develop out of it.

Max and Lacey were settling in well, and Rachel had a perpetual smile on her face. Obviously Denver PD Officer West was keeping her very happy. Flynn, Willow, and their daughter Raven were thriving. Flynn obviously loved being a very hands on dad, and doted on his baby girl. Chad thought that Flynn was a good example for John Palmer. The once closed off former SEAL took to fatherhood like a duck to water and loved it.

Chad missed seeing Zeke. The big guy worked graveyard shift now so that he could help his fiancée with the Frog Dog Bar and Grill and raise their son Drew. Gabe and Julie Carter fit the group so well, it seemed like they'd always been part of LNF.

Everyone seemed good and settled into their happy relationships except him.

Now, he loved Lora, there was no doubt about that, but he missed her. He knew from watching his parents' long and happy marriage that you needed a lot of contact to make the relationship work. It had been weeks since they'd talked about anything more important than Mercy or her classes, let alone actually made love. Chad had let her know more than once that he needed affection, but she'd seemed lost in her own tiredness and drive to learn the business.

Something needed to change.

Nothing was going to change until he talked to her though.

Chad was glad that Duncan was such a strategic thinker because less than five minutes after he left the office Palmer called to tell him the guy showed up at the client's place of work. Chad parked his truck and jumped out, long legs eating up the distance to the front door. The suspect, Jerry Wallace, had broken several protection orders between him and his ex-girlfriend, Tiki. Now, the company where Tiki worked was filing a 'leave the premises' warning. The next time Jerry showed up the cops would be called and he would be taken to jail on trespassing charges.

Chad needed to make sure the guy understood everything about his situation. Hopefully they could get this done and all move on with their days.

The receptionist, Penny, waved when she saw him, and motioned to the hallway to the right. "Break room," she whispered, her brown eyes wide with fear.

Tipping his hat, Chad strode down the hallway. Without hesitation he pushed through the swinging door, his gaze latching onto the couple in the back corner. No one else was in the room. Tiki, a petite dark-haired girl with a lot of make-up on, stood against a vending machine, arms crossed over her stomach, an obvious sign that she wanted no part of the blond-haired kid in front of her. He wasn't much taller than the girl, but Chad could see his ego from here.

Why did some little men always have to overcompensate and be assholes?

The male reached out to finger the girl's hair and Chad thought it was a good time to interject himself. Smoothly, he handed the kid the manila envelope and gave the girl his back. "Hold this for me buddy. Oh, and just so you know, you've now been served notice that you are no longer permitted on these premises. If you come here again, you will be arrested for trespassing. Denver PD has a copy of the order I just gave you."

Red began to suffuse the kid's face, and Chad realized he was older than he looked. Probably at least twenty-five or twenty-six. Old enough to know better.

"What the fuck are you talking about cowboy?" he snarled.

"You have been served notice that you are no longer allowed on these premises," he repeated, more slowly. "Do you need me to say it a third time?"

The young man scowled and ripped open the envelope, then scanned the papers inside. "This is bullshit. I'm allowed to come see my girl."

"Well, actually," Chad started, but he didn't get a chance to finish. The girl had stepped to the side to confront the young man.

"I'm not your girl," she yelled. "I keep telling you that. We had *one date*, and you refused to listen to a word I said. I'm done with you, Jerry. I'm tired of you threatening me like you've got some kind of right to me."

Chad knew the guy was going to do something stupid, so when he reached out to slap the girl, he struck Chad's shoulder instead. That seemed to piss him off even more though. Stepping back, he reared back a fist.

Chad would have laughed if it hadn't been so sad. He had at least eight inches on the guy, and probably a hundred pounds. He let the dude throw the punch, simply because it was that much more they had on tape. Gunny Palmer was recording everything right now, he had no doubt.

The punch barely rocked his head. The kid blinked when

he realized he hadn't done anything to Chad, and took a step back in preparation of getting his ass kicked.

"Are you done throwing your tantrum, Sugar?" Chad asked him.

Fists clenched, the kid spun away with a snarl and stalked out of the room.

Licking at his mouth, Chad realized he had a busted lip. He looked up at the camera in the far corner for a moment for documentation purposes then took the handful of napkins the girl was shoving at him. There were tears rolling down her face now, streaking her makeup.

"I kept telling him to leave, but he wouldn't listen. I knew he wouldn't. That's why I told my boss he needed a security door, but he didn't listen either."

"He listened, actually." Chad swiped at the split lip, but it seemed to have quit bleeding. "We've been watching for the past few days, waiting for Jerry to show up."

She blinked and looked around. "Really?"

He nodded, but didn't bother pointing out the new cameras they had installed. "If he comes around again, call the cops. The receptionist has a copy of the order as well, and a new lock is being added to the front vestibule door, which can be controlled remotely. I suggest you update your restraining order information so that this doesn't happen again."

The girl nodded emphatically. "I'll do that. Thank you so much."

With a wave, Chad left the room. The receptionist was wide-eyed but grinning now when he stopped at her desk. "I heard everything. Thank you. You guys did such an excellent job. I didn't expect him to react that way, but you did. Well done."

Chad grinned at her, till the split in his lip protested. "Thank you, ma'am."

She ducked down and reached for something in a drawer, then handed him a wet baby wipe. "You have blood on your chin."

Chad scrubbed where she instructed, but apparently didn't get it, because she reached out to guide his hand where it needed to go. She glanced up at him from beneath her eyelashes, and Chad suddenly felt a little uncomfortable. Was she flirting with him?

"You know, maybe we can grab a beer sometime." The woman smiled at him.

Chad appreciated the interest. It had been a long time since he'd played the field.

"I thank you, Penny, but I'm in a relationship."

Penny glanced down at his left hand and he suddenly wished he had a band there. Surprisingly, she didn't even wince when she saw his injured hand. She hadn't winced at the scars that ran up his neck either. Instead, she looked him in the eye and smiled again. "That's fine, then. Thank you for telling me."

She turned back to her desk. "Figures," she laughed. "First hot guy I asked out since my breakup and he's taken."

Chad grinned at her. "It was a great line. You did it exactly right, I promise. If I wasn't taken I would absolutely have gone out with you."

She laughed lightly, and Chad wondered who he could set her up with. Surely one of his buddies needed a nice woman. He'd have to think on it.

"Thanks for the ego boost, Penny. I appreciate it. Let us know if you need anything else."

With a final tip of his hat, he left.

He chuckled to himself as he walked to the truck. Without being egotistical, he knew he was good looking enough. Women watched him a lot. The damn arm shut most of them down pretty quickly though.

The gnarly thing was hard for him to look at, let alone other people. Once again, he wondered if he shouldn't just get the damn thing chopped off. Even a prosthetic would probably look better than this thing. He turned it over, looking at the clawed fingers. They'd gotten so tight recently that he knew he was going to have to go in to have the contracting scars released soon. He'd probably need another skin graft, which sometimes hurt as bad as the original injury.

Even as beat up as his hand was, though, it still had some mobility. Probably more than he'd have with a prosthetic. Sighing, he climbed into the truck and pulled the door shut behind him. It was good enough to do that, so he'd hang onto it for a while.

John grinned at him when he returned to the office. "Hey, Buttercup. Still charming the ladies, I see."

Snorting, Chad shrugged good-naturedly. "What can I say? Did you get all that?"

John scowled at him, his dark eyes narrowing. "Seriously? Do I look like I just started this fucking job?"

Chad shrugged. "Well, you are getting pretty old."

He ducked the roll of black electric tape as it sailed past his head. "And your aim is off. Dude, I was joking, but damn, that's sad."

He took off running before John exited the office. "Good thing I didn't wear my sidearm today, Lowell."

Chad laughed as he ducked into the exercise room. Gunny Palmer pretended he was offended, but the jokes were all in good fun. The two of them went back many years. They'd seen good times and plenty of bad ones as well. Now that they'd gained some maturity, it seemed like things were rolling more their way now.

Well, John's life seemed to be rolling well now. Shannon loved him so much it hurt to look at them together. And they had two kids coming. They didn't know the sex yet, but John was forecasting gloom and doom, bemoaning the fact that he would be the only male in the house when the *girls* were born.

Chad thought she would have boys, like John's long-lost brother Jaime had said before he'd disappeared again.

He snorted as he walked over to the bank of lockers and spun the combination lock. What a crazy year it had been so far. Only seven months to go.

Would Lora marry him this year?

Honestly, he wanted to drag her away from everything. Away from school and business and her damn office, just to give her time to gain some perspective. She was locked into the same groove for days at a time, and it had to be hard on her body. As well as her mind.

She was so hard working at making them a better life that she was losing sight of the one she had.

CHAPTER 3

LORA RUBBED her eyes and yawned, glancing at the clock. No way! Where had the day gone? It was almost time for her to pick Mercy up from school.

Pushing away from the desk, she looked down at herself. Sleep pants and t-shirt were fine for computer work, but not when she went out in public. Were they? Wafting her shirt, she cringed. No, she definitely needed a shower and fresh clothes.

Lora hurried through the cleaning. She blew her hair dry enough that she could pull it back into a ponytail, then brushed her teeth. She had just enough time to grab a banana from the basket and a bottle of water from the fridge before she bolted out the door, car keys in hand. She paused long enough to set the house alarm with the little key fob, and she was in the car, heading down the street toward Mercy's school.

Man, she must be early, she decided a few minutes later. There was no congestion around the school. When she pulled into the main entrance, she knew something was wrong. There were cars in the lot, but no school buses and no kids. At almost the same moment, her phone let off a blaring alarm.

"Perimeter Breach. Perimeter Breach."

Lora fumbled the phone, so thankful that there was no one behind her. Flicking through the sign-in, she looked at the remote control camera feed.

The front door of her house stood wide open.

Pure terror bolted through her. It was like those nightmare years when Derek was alive, all over again. Worrying about what was going to happen when she was away from the house, wondering where her daughter was every second of the day. It was why she had taken the job at the school years ago; so that she could be close to Mercy in case anything happened.

She gasped in a breath and steered the car to the side of the school driveway, her heart thundering in her ears. Where was Mercy?

The phone rang in her hand. Chad.

"What's going on, darlin'?"

Lora dragged in a breath. "I don't know. There's no one at the school. Do you have Mercy?"

There was a long silence on the end of the line. "Mercy stayed home today, Lora. When I left she was still in bed, and you were on the computer. They had a teacher in-service today, remember?"

No, she didn't. *Fuck!*

"I need to get home, then. She must be home. And she must have opened the door after I set the alarm."

"Okay. Do you need me to come get you?"

"No, I'll be fine."

Now that she knew where her daughter was she would be. She swung the car around.

"I'll meet you there, Lora."

She hung up without saying anything.

The ten minutes it took her to get home were interminable. Panic raced through her when she saw the familiar white Denver PD cruiser parked in her drive, till she realized the officer sitting on the front steps with Mercy was Dean West, Rachel's boyfriend. They were both eating popsicles, like nothing had happened.

Lora leapt out of the car and hurried across the drive. She squatted down and hugged Mercy to her, trying not to cry.

"Mom, my popsicle," she protested.

Lora let her go and stepped back, swiping beneath her eyes.

Dean gave her a considering look and lifted a brow. "You doing okay, Lora?"

She shook her head, fighting the tears. She'd really messed up today, and if she was offered kindness she would break down completely. If her daughter had been harmed in any way she would never have forgiven herself.

When Chad pulled into the driveway, her breath hitched in her throat. He was such a good, concerned father. If he yelled at her right now she so wouldn't blame him.

Chad crossed the driveway and hunkered down in front of Mercy. "Hey, darlin'."

"Hey," she responded, licking the purple juice from her lips.

"Nice seeing Dean today, huh?"

She nodded happily, nibbling around the stick. "He should have brought Rachel too, though."

"I will next time," Dean promised her.

The young, heavily built man looked up at Chad as he bit into the other half of the purple popsicle. "I happened to be in the area when I heard there was something going on at your house. Mercy met me on the porch. I checked the area real quick, but Mercy said she'd seen you drive away." His gaze flicked to Lora. "She just forgot about the alarm being on. So, dispatch called your security company back and assured them we were on scene and everything was secure. We thought we would munch a popsicle while we waited for you to get back."

Lora straightened her spine. "I appreciate that. You're welcome to come over for a treat anytime."

Mercy nodded her head, wiping her mouth on the long sleeve of her shirt. "Anytime."

Dean cleaned off the stick and handed it to Mercy to go throw away inside the house. "I need to get back to work, kiddo. Thanks for sharing with me. Maybe this weekend we can meet you at the park or something."

With a hug around his neck, she nodded. "Okay. Bye, Dean."

Standing, Dean moved closer to Chad. "I don't think she even realized what craziness she set off. You might talk to her about the alarm system."

Chad reached out and shook his hand. Lora moved closer to take his hand as well. "I'm sorry, Dean. I just got my days mixed up. I forgot about the teacher in-service."

He shrugged. "It happens. No big deal. I'll see y'all later."

With a final wave he climbed into the cruiser, maneuvered around the two vehicles parked behind him and accelerated away.

Lora looked up at Chad, trying to see censure or condemnation in his expression, but all she saw was sadness. And a tightness around his lips. Without saying anything to her, he jumped up the steps to follow Mercy.

That brushoff hurt more than anything. Even as subtle as it was, she could tell she'd disappointed him. She'd disappointed herself as well.

Taking a deep breath she climbed the shallow steps and crossed to the front door. Chad and Mercy were in the kitchen. Her daughter was washing her hands while Chad leaned his butt against the center island. Lora could tell that he was getting ready to speak to the girl.

Mercy didn't smile when she turned around, drying her hands on a tea-towel. "I did something wrong, didn't I?"

Chad reached out to rest a hand on her shoulder. "Not wrong, exactly. I don't think you understand how serious that door alarm is. Even though it doesn't go off here, it does in other places. So even though you didn't hear anything, there were a lot of people that started running. Dean is a friend, so he responded to this call, but if he hadn't been on duty there would have been police cars in the driveway with lights and sirens on. John would have been here with a team. It hasn't been that long since everything happened in Texas, and people are still worried about us as a family."

Mercy nodded, her long blond hair hanging over her face. Lora didn't like to see her so despondent.

"It was my fault," she blurted. "I didn't even think when I left to go get you at school. The teacher in-service didn't even occur to me." She glanced at the fridge, feeling guilty. Now that she had remembered, she also remembered all the reminders Chad had left. Fridge, on her desk blotter. There was even a post-it note in her day planner.

Mercy glanced up at her. "It's okay, Mom. I know you were busy. I was trying to be extra quiet today."

Lora felt like roadkill. She was in the wrong but her daughter was trying to make her feel better. She drew her into her arms, running a hand through Mercy's knotted hair. "No worries, sweetheart. We both just have to pay more attention next time, right?"

Mercy nodded against her, her fist curled against her chest.

For the first time in an hour, Lora took a deep breath. Her daughter was fine in her arms and everything was right in the world.

Well, almost everything. Her gaze drifted to Chad, who had his arms crossed as he leaned against the island. Their gazes connected and she searched for that reassurance he always gave her, but it wasn't there right now. His icy blue eyes were remote as he watched them together.

The cell phone in her pocket went off, drawing her attention. Heaving a sigh, Mercy pulled away. She didn't know if it was the stress of the day making her focus, or what, but Lora took note of the movement. Suddenly, with total clarity, she realized that she had been interrupted the same way many times before, and Mercy pulled away the same way.

Before she disengaged completely, Lora snagged her hand. Mercy looked up at her in surprise. "I love you, sweetie."

"I know, Mom."

Chad ruffled her hair as she walked away toward the stairs and Lora realized it had been cut recently. It fell halfway down her daughter's back, cut straight across. It made her look taller.

Lora turned toward the sink, thinking about the time that had passed. It had been over a year since Derek had attacked them on Chad's family ranch.

"We need to talk, Lora."

With sigh, she turned around. Chad hadn't moved. He stood there in the shining light of her beautiful kitchen, outshining everything around him. He was the most beautiful man she'd ever seen, even with the damaged left hand. She didn't even notice it anymore. Or the scars on his face and neck. They had faded almost to nothing. And you couldn't even tell he was missing his lower left leg. He moved as if he didn't even have a prosthetic.

He was truly her hero. When she and Mercy had stood alone against the world, he had been there to support them.

Maybe that was why it was so shocking to feel the anger he held in check rolling off him.

Before they could say anything, her phone rang again. True anger twisted Chad's face before he turned away. Stalking to the refrigerator, he jerked open the door, grabbing a bottle of water before he walked out of the room. He went through the French doors and into the back yard.

Lora felt like she was walking on quicksand. And it had only taken an hour to change everything.

She glanced at the screen. William in New York. Sighing, she took the call.

CHAPTER 4

CHAD KNEW he needed to get a grip on the anger that was building, but he was so frustrated. Today could have been very bad. He trusted in Mercy's safety inside the house, and in general really. He didn't think there was any lingering danger from the long dead Derek Malone. But he knew how Lora would react at the slightest hiccup in routine. Yes, they'd dealt with Derek, but Lora still lived as if he were just around the corner. She was usually hyper vigilant around Mercy, treating the eight year old as if she couldn't think for herself.

But the girl was growing. She was already a brilliant kid, and the experiences she'd had made her more cautious than the average kid her age. But even she was beginning to feel stifled under Lora's drastic swings. They were living in a situation that was not good for Mercy. She was either clamped down on and restricted or ignored because her mother was overwhelmed by other things.

Handsome the bear now occupied a shelf in Mercy's room. Chad was impressed that she'd had the gumption to let go of him herself. Actually, being around other kids her age had probably motivated that.

Mercy had come to him the other night and asked him if she thought her mother would let her attend a friend's birthday party. Not wanting to sugar-coat it, Chad had told her he wasn't sure, but that he would ask for her. He hadn't yet had a chance to do that, and after this incident he didn't know if he could right now. It might be one of those things that he needed to ask forgiveness for rather than permission.

Chad dropped down into one of the Adirondack chairs on the back patio, hoping that serenity would find him. He chuckled to himself. That wasn't likely right now.

His cell phone rang in his pocket, and he was surprised to see Cheyenne's name on the contact. "Hey, sis, what are you up to?"

"Chad, you might want to think about coming home. Daddy's in the hospital. He took a spill from his horse when he was roping a calf. Not sure about the details but Brock thinks he might have had a heart attack."

Chad was glad he was sitting down. "Wait, what? A heart attack?"

"Yes," she sighed. "I'm sorry to call you like this, but I can't get a hold of Emily. Brock is on his way to be in Amarillo with Mama and Daddy now, but with the girls I can't just leave. Payton is on duty with the squad right now, but as soon as she goes off shift she'll come stay with my girls. Then I'll drive down."

"Okay, I'll call Duncan and get time off. What happened to him?"

"I'm not sure," she said. "Brock was with him when it happened and I think he may have done CPR on him. He was on the range so they took him by Lifestar helicopter straight to Amarillo. Brock is still driving mom up but he should get there any time."

Chad's heart was racing with them, hoping they got there as soon as possible. "It'll take me at least seven hours to get there, unless I can hop a flight. I'll let you know after I talk to Lora and Duncan."

"Okay. Love you. I'm sorry to have to call you like this."

"That's okay. I don't think there's any way to make it easier."

"True. I'll see you when you get there."

Chad jumped up and ran into the house, his mind churning. Lora still stood in the kitchen, ear to her phone. She must have felt the urgency, though, because she made her excuses and hung up. "What's wrong?"

"I'm heading to Amarillo. Cheyenne just called. They think Dad had a heart attack."

Lora gasped, her eyes filling with concern. She rushed to him, resting her hand on his arm. "Oh, no. Are there any details? Has he been seen?"

Chad shook his head. "All I know is Brock was with him on the range, and they had to fly him in the emergency helicopter to Amarillo. Mom and Brock are on their way up, and Cheyenne will go up as soon as she has someone to watch the kids."

She reached up to cup his cheek. "Okay, what do we need to do?"

Chad's throat constricted. Apparently he wasn't totally wallpaper. She did see him sometimes.

"I need to call Duncan, but that's just to let him know where I'm going. Then I need to decide if I'm flying or driving."

"By the time you get to the airport, catch a flight that may or may not be there, plus a connector, rent a car and drive there, you might as well just drive."

He nodded, knowing she was correct. "Yes, I agree. I'm going to go pack a bag."

"And I'll have Mercy pack a bag."

Chad looked at her sharply. "You're going with me?"

Lora frowned at him, her green eyes narrowed. "Of course we are. We love Garrett as much as you do. Something like this you need family around you. Francine will, even if Garrett doesn't know we're there."

Blinking, he nodded. "I agree. Didn't know if you'd be able to drag yourself away."

Lora winced a little, and her eyes got a little unfocused, like she was thinking about everything she had to do. "I'll make it work," she said firmly. "Let's move."

Chad called Duncan, but it was just a formality. Boss man knew how important family was. He needed to know what was going on with some of the smaller cases, though.

"We wrapped the Watt-tech case and all the paperwork has been filed," Chad told him. "Brian Calvert is wrapping up his forensic accounting case for the country singer Henry Bright, too."

"Did he figure out who'd been embezzling from him?"

"Yeah," Chad sighed. "Exactly who Brian thought it was at the beginning. The asshole told Bright he was squirreling it away as a nest egg for them."

Duncan choked out a laugh. "That's a good one. Anything else I need to know about?"

"Not that I can think of," Chad told him honestly. "If anything occurs to me I'll let you know."

"Sounds good. Keep me updated on Garrett's condition and take the time you need."

Chad packed several days' worth of clothes in a duffle and grabbed his spare prosthetic leg and his blade. He had no idea how long they would be down there, but he needed to be prepared for anything. In his gut, he had a feeling it would not be a quick trip. Dad still did a lot around the ranch. If they were short he could maybe step in for a while.

The thought of his father not being a part of the ranch seemed desperately wrong.

Mercy came in through the doorway, tears in her eyes. "Is Grampa Lowell going to be okay?"

Chad knelt down before her, giving her good eye contact. "I don't know darlin'. I sure hope so. Sounds like he's really sick right now. Do you have everything packed?"

She nodded her head. "Mom's checking it. And I'm supposed to go to the basement and make sure everything is turned off."

"That's a good thing for you to do. Is your tablet charged? We're going to be in the truck for a while. Then we might be at the hospital for a while too."

Wincing, she raced out the door to check. Chad heaved a breath, wondering what he was forgetting as well. Another sleeve for his stump. Cream for the skin of his left hand, though it didn't seem like it was doing much good anymore. It was more contracted than ever.

Walking from the room he grabbed his tablet as well as the phone charger from his side of the bed.

Within fifteen minutes they were walking out the door. Mercy had her bag and a pillow in hand so that she could sleep. They would be driving into the night.

Two hours into the drive south, Cheyenne called. "So, apparently Dad was chasing after a calf. Brock remembers looking over and seeing him grab his chest, rein up the horse and fall off. Unfortunately, he landed on his arm, breaking it. The doctors are in with him now and I'm on my way there. Sounds like he did have a heart attack and he's going to have stents put in to repair the blockages they have found. Brock says the doctors seem pretty casual about it because they do it all the time."

Chad felt a knot of tension ease in his gut. "So it sounds like he's going to be okay..."

"Yeah," she sighed. "I think so. He's too hard-headed not to be. Sounds like he's going to need surgery on the arm, too, but that will happen after the heart stents."

"Damn," Chad said. "Thanks for the update. We should be there within about four hours."

"Okay. Be safe."

Lora's hand was on his shoulder, rubbing, calming. "So he'll be okay?"

"Yeah, I think so. The heart attack led to the broken arm, so he's going to have to slow down for a while. They're putting stents into the blocked arteries, then they'll work on the arm later."

She winced and shook her head. "Poor Garrett. This is going to put him out of commission for a while."

"Yeah," Chad agreed.

It was seriously going to put a crimp in the old man's tail not being able to use his arm, let alone whatever damage he took from the heart attack.

They finished the drive in quiet. Once the light faded Mercy played with her tablet for a while before going to sleep. Chad glanced over at Lora. Her hands were folded in her lap and there was a somber expression on her face. She'd done a few things on her phone before putting it away. "I'm sorry to drag you away from everything."

She looked at him, frowning. The light had faded from the sky and the only illumination was from the dash of the truck. "Don't be sorry. This wasn't your fault. It wasn't anyone's fault. It was just one of those things that happen and have to be dealt with."

Chad blinked at her, then looked back at the road. He'd thought for sure that she'd be pissed about her schedule being messed up. Or her schooling. She'd been so single-minded recently.

"We'll see how he is when we get there. Maybe you can get back to everything in a day or so."

She gave a slight shrug. "We'll see. If I'm needed here I'll stay."

That she would even make the offer made him happy. For a long time he'd been feeling like second fiddle, and feeling guilty for that on top of everything.

Conversation drifted away, but it didn't feel as awkward as it had been before. When Lora's head began to bob, he motioned to his thigh. "Why don't you lie down here?"

Without a word she maneuvered herself to lie across the bench seat, her head on his leg. Without even thinking about it, Chad reached down and stroked her hair from her face. Within seconds she'd fallen asleep, but he continued to touch her, just because he could.

CHAPTER 5

THE HOSPITAL in Amarillo was surprisingly busy, considering it was one a.m. The woman at the reception desk smiled at them warmly and checked Garrett's whereabouts on the computer in front of her. "Room 532," she told them, then pointed to the hallway with the elevators.

Chad's heart thumped as they climbed, and it wasn't because he carried the drowsy Mercy. His father was such a vital part of everyone's lives, he just couldn't imagine losing him.

Being in a hospital also put him on edge. The smells and the bright lights played havoc with his mind. Zeke, during one of his stays, had once joked about having more PTSD from the hospitals themselves than the injuries they were getting care for, and it was eerily true.

Cheyenne saw them first because she was standing at the nurse's station on the fifth floor. Her eyes turned glossy with tears, and even though he held Mercy he held an arm out for Cheyenne's hug. She grabbed him and wouldn't let go. He kissed the top of her wavy auburn hair. "He's gonna be okay. You know that."

She nodded against him, then pulled away to swipe the tears from her cheeks. Turning to Lora she pulled her into a hug as well.

Chad was surprised to see Lora's eyes fill with tears as well.

"Come on, y'all," he growled. "He's not that bad. They're going to fix him, right?"

Cheyenne nodded. "Yes, he already went in for the repair. It's done. They're going to let him recover for a couple days, then they'll repair the arm. He woke up for a little bit, long enough to talk to Mama, then he went back to sleep. She's in there with him now."

Tension rolled out of his shoulders. "That's good news. He's a tough old bird. This isn't something that will keep him down for long."

When Chad saw his father a few minutes later, though, he wasn't so sure. Garrett's pallor was positively deathly, even with the oxygen cannula beneath his nose and the lights dimmed for the night.

His mother looked up with a smile and leaned up for his hug. "You made good time from Denver. Is my grandbaby out there too or is it just you?"

"All three of us came down."

His mother's graying brows shot into her hair. "Lora came? Really? I knew she was busy..."

He nodded, not wanting to get into the issue. He looked back at his father. "What have the doctors said?"

She sighed, rubbing her husband's hand on the mattress. "They had to put in three stents for blocked arteries, but the procedure was easy. No issues at all. Garrett is not going to like what they prescribe, though. More salads, less fried food like he sneaks away for in town. Pills to keep his levels in control."

Chad winced. Garrett Lowell believed in living life the

way you wanted to. Strictures did not play into his day-to-day life. It was only within the past couple of years that his mother had started trying to eat healthier. Garrett had grumbled, not liking the changes. For Mama, though, he'd modified a few things. Garrett would do anything for her.

But it hadn't been enough, apparently.

"So, what's the plan?"

His mother sighed, suddenly looking more tired than he could ever remember her being. "He's come around a couple of times but they have him on pain meds for the arm. It's broken in three places and will need a plate to fix, as well as several screws."

Chad looked at his dad's right arm. It was bandaged from shoulder to fingertips and propped up on a mound of pillows on the bed. Yeah, if it was broken that badly it would need internal support.

He was going to be out of commission for a while. At least he was left-handed. That was one small bright spot in the situation. He'd still be able to do most things for himself.

"Once Brock saw he was out of surgery and doing okay he headed back to the Blue Star. We've had a few late calves that haven't done well and need some extra care. As well as a couple of hands that chose now to take vacation. Well, one is helping his mama move, I'll give him that, and it was planned. But the other won him some money on a scratch off ticket and headed for Mexico." Mama shook her head. "It's been a crazy week and it's barely started."

Ranching was hard work. Chad remembered those never ending days. Being bloody and as foul as it was possible for a human to be, then moving on to the next calf. So saddle-sore your balls were chapped. But even with all the nastiness, seeing bright-eyed calves on the ground or nursing mama cow almost made it worth the aggravation.

They had enough money to pay men to do it now, but

Chad knew that his brother Brock loved to be in control of everything. He would be on the range every moment he could be, or at the very least in the paddocks with his prized Quarter horses.

Chad could almost envy him his simple lifestyle.

Looking at his dad, though, he found himself worrying about the ranch.

≈

BROCK LOOKED at the lit phone screen. Payton.

Unplugging the charger he swiped the screen and lifted it to his ear. "Hey."

"Hey. Are you guys all right? I haven't heard from Cheyenne in a while."

He sighed, sinking into the truck seat. He'd been getting a little drowsy driving back to the ranch, so he was kind of glad she'd called, though it was a little strange. They would probably be considered friends, though she very rarely called him. These were extenuating circumstances, though. "Everyone is fine. Dad is out of surgery and seems to be improving already. His arm will be worked on in a couple days. Mama is a little frantic but controlling it well. Cheyenne is a bit of a basket case."

"And how are you doing," she asked softly.

That question kind of stalled him out, and the silence lengthened. Very few people had ever asked him how he was doing. They just assumed that if he was working he was fine.

Brock wasn't sure if it was the dark of the night and the lonely road or what, or some faint connection he had with Payton, but he wanted a little reassurance. "I'm okay, I think. I'll admit watching him go down was one of the worst things I've ever seen."

The sequence of events replayed in his mind as if it were

a movie playing right in front of his eyes. Dad had taken off after a calf, his dark bay surging strongly beneath him. He'd lifted the rope to snag him, but the shot went wild as his father clutched at his chest. Brock had seen the fear in his father's eyes, the shock, as he lost his balance and rolled off the horse, landing heavily on the ground. Dad had made no effort to break his fall.

The few seconds it had taken Brock to bolt across the yards separating them, leap from his own horse and bend over his father had seemed like years. Rolling him over, he'd seen the unnatural way Dad's arm had bent, and he'd had to fight nausea.

"I think you did everything perfectly," Payton told him. "If he'd been alone chasing that calf we would have had a very different outcome."

Yes, Brock had thought about that too, and it downright terrified him.

"I did what they told us in that damn first aid and CPR class you made us sit through."

Payton laughed on the other end of the line. "I don't think you can call it that any more considering it just saved your father's life."

Brock sighed as he maneuvered around a slow-moving semi. "Yeah, I guess not."

"I'm very thankful you were there, Brock. Garrett is as much of a father figure to me as my own, and if something had happened to him it would have been devastating. For everyone. You just never know when your time is up, you know?"

"Yeah."

That was very true.

He hung up from Payton feeling a little more relaxed about what had happened. Initially, when she'd suggested that they needed to update their first aid certifications, he'd shrugged her off. But she'd persisted, telling him that her supervisor would come out any time to train them. The brat had finally worn him down, and he was glad she had. He, Jackson and ten of the hands had only been certified for a few months. And now this had happened.

Her parting words stayed with him. Time *was* passing so fast.

CHAPTER 6

THERE WAS a hotel directly across the street from the hospital, visible from the waiting room. Lora called and asked what they had available. The young woman described several rooms, then the suites. Lora booked them a suite with two bedrooms and a sitting room, as well as a small kitchenette. She doubted she would be cooking any gourmet meals or anything, but it might be nice to have the setup just in case. The fridge would come in handy if nothing else.

Cheyenne had already rented a room in the same hotel, just so Francine could have a place to go when she needed to. Their mother didn't want to leave Garrett right now, but she would eventually.

"I just can't believe he did this," Cheyenne murmured again.

Lora reached over and squeezed her hand, something she'd done a couple of times already. Cheyenne was one of the strongest women she knew in real life, but seeing her father knocked down so hard was shocking.

Lora could empathize. Garrett had always seemed to be one of the strongest men she'd known as well, next to Chad.

"It's not like he had a choice in the matter, Cheyenne. Nobody chooses to have a heart attack."

Chad's sister grimaced. "I know. He's just been such a bull for so long."

"And he'll be a bull about his recovery as well. You have to have faith that he will."

Cheyenne nodded, leaning her shoulder into Lora's for a moment. "So, how is conquering the business world coming along?"

Lora grimaced. "Not so great. We've had some growth issues recently."

Cheyenne tilted her head, her smart eyes focusing on Lora's expression. "Like what?"

She struggled with what to say. Cheyenne seemed so put together. Even raising her three girls and working full time as a teacher, she seemed to have all her ducks in a row. "I'm struggling with splitting family time and work time. Right now, school and learning from William is really taking my focus. So much so that we had a security issue yesterday."

Lora told her what had happened. Cheyenne listened carefully, then shrugged. "Stuff like that happens. It was an accident. Nobody was hurt or even really in danger."

Yes, that was true to an extent. "Dean responded to the alarm and he was great, but I could tell Chad was pissed."

Cheyenne pulled back. "Chad pissed? No way!"

Lora nodded, folding her arms across her chest. "Not screaming mad, just ... quietly steaming. He's losing patience with me."

Cheyenne sighed, reaching for Lora's hand. "Chad is the epitome of patience, you know that. Heck, it's been more than a year since he asked you to marry him, and I never thought he'd wait for anyone this long. I might have thought once that he'd sweep you off your feet and straight to Vegas in no time but that wouldn't be right for you, either one of you. He has the willpower to wait for you forever, because he loves you. But maybe if he's not getting any acknowledgement for what he's doing, it might make him a little frustrated."

Lora's mouth slackened. Had it actually been *more than a year* since he'd proposed to her and Mercy? Holy smokes, it *had—* how did a year just go by so fast? Her weighty guilt gained more heft. They'd been together even longer.

Then she thought about Mercy's haircut, and the strange pair of shoes she'd been wearing the other day. Chad had done those things for her, as a father should. He'd been stepping up the entire time, but Cheyenne was right. Lora hadn't let him know enough she'd seen him, and what he was doing for the family.

She ran a hand over her face, realizing as she did so that she hadn't even looked at herself recently. She probably had old makeup beneath her eyes. Tucking her hair behind her ear, she glanced at Cheyenne, who looked beautiful at any time of night or day. Even now her dark auburn hair was twisted into some kind of casual bun that looked more perfect than anything Lora could have tried to do. And her pale skin was so flawless. Lora wasn't sure how she kept it so creamy in the Texas dryness. In spite of the late hour, her blue eyes were bright and only appeared a little tired. Cheyenne always looked like she was ready to go on a date or teach a class.

Lora looked down at the gray sweater she wore and the maroon-colored long-sleeved t-shirt beneath it. Definitely casual. Too casual. But this was what she wore every day, every single day. Ugh, she was in a rut.

Did Chad wished she was as made up as Cheyenne?

It didn't matter. They had other things to think about right now.

"Do the doctors have any idea when your dad might get out?"

Cheyenne shook her head. "No, but they said at least a few days, if not more depending upon how he does. Daddy is sixty this year. He may think he can still ride and wrestle like these younger kids, but he's starting to slow down. Brock said he'd been roping calves with the rest of them when this happened." She winced, looking at Lora out of the corner of her eyes. "I hate to say it, but maybe this is a good thing. Maybe it will slow him down a little and make him take a step back. He should enjoy life rather than work all the time. Brock has been dying to take control of the ranch. He has some wonderful ideas, but Daddy hasn't given in. Mama would love for him to slow down too. I know she's always wanted to travel, but Daddy was always anchored down with the ranch."

"Where would your mother go if she had the chance?" Lora asked, curious.

Cheyenne looked at her in surprise. "Oh, you haven't figured it out? She would love to go to Paris and see the Eiffel Tower, wander the romantic streets, drink coffee in a little bistro. It's been a dream of hers her entire life. Have you ever been in their bedroom?"

Lora shook her head, intrigued.

"Oh, it's decorated like a Paris boutique hotel. Gauzy drapes and table skirts. Her winter bedspread is a beautiful heavy red brocade. She has the Eiffel Tower on her wallpaper. Daddy always complained about it being too frou-frou, but he loves Mama and he decorated it for her like that. He found a news article she'd cut out about places to stay, or something, and he did it up for her. Made her bawl like a baby. He's promised her Paris for years, but they've never gotten around to it."

That was very sweet. The two of them loved each other

very much. Maybe Cheyenne was right. Perhaps they would be able to slow down now for a while.

Hopefully she and Chad would have a long-lived marriage like that.

They just needed to get married first.

Something else to feel guilty about. They'd postponed it because of her schedule. Her never-ending, being-tugged-in-nine-million-directions schedule.

That wasn't really an excuse though. If she could make time to talk to William on the phone about a personnel issue, she should certainly be able to see to the needs of her family. Her phone buzzed in her pocket, but she refused to look at the accumulating demands. London was five hours ahead of New York, so they'd already started work at the London branch of Malone. As soon as the New York office opened it would be buzzing even more. At some point she needed to check in and tell William what was going on.

Mercy snuffled in her sleep and shifted. She'd curled up on a little padded bench, with her jacket over top of her and her head resting on Lora's purse. Her blonde hair was over her face a little and Lora wanted to go over and brush it away, but it would be better to just let her sleep while she could. Blinking, she widened her own eyes, trying to fight her own tiredness. It wasn't working.

Chad had to be worn out, too. After working all day, running home for Mercy, then driving all night, he had to be wearing down. As if her thoughts had conjured him from the air, he walked into the room, looking tall and gorgeous in spite of the hour. He took off his tan cowboy hat and when he sat down, dropped it into the seat beside him.

Lora waited, knowing that he would fill her in as soon as possible.

"He's sleeping, but he did wake enough to look at me and squeeze my hand. Mom refuses to leave until he rouses completely, and I think that's best. If he wakes up and she's not there he's going to worry, and he doesn't need that right now."

"No, he doesn't," she agreed.

"Cheyenne, if you want, why don't you go get some sleep at the hotel? And when you come back in a few hours we'll swap off with you, and try to get Mom to leave. There's no budging her right now, but you're the persuasive one. If you're fresh and she's not maybe it'll be easier getting her to go rest."

Cheyenne nodded, beginning to gather up her things. "I think that sounds like a fabulous idea. I haven't slept for two days. Savannah had a migraine through the night so I was up with her."

"Is she okay?" Chad asked.

Cheyenne shrugged. "I think so. She gets them sometimes when she stresses out too much. She's my little prodigy and school has been hard for her this year. She's actually having to do homework." She grinned and winked at Chad.

"I don't think I like what you're insinuating there, sister."

Cheyenne laughed and moved to give him a hug. "I'll be back by nine."

They waved her goodbye and she was gone. Lora worked her arm through his and leaned into his shoulder. "Are you going to last that long?"

Chad snorted, glancing at her. "Yeah, I can. Unfortunately, I've gotten good at catching cat naps in hospital waiting rooms."

Lora cocked her head at him. "Really?"

"I've gone with Zeke to several of his last reconstructive surgeries. And Harper. Duncan was the one most recently in the chop shop."

Lora grimaced at the slang, even though it was a little appropriate.

"That's right," she murmured. "You know, you forget looking at them what all they've been through. You're a good man to go with them like that."

Chad shrugged, holding up his own scarred hand. "They've been there for me before, many times, and I'm sure they will again. I'm going to have to go get this cut again."

Lora leaned forward to look into his face. "Are you really?"

"Yeah. It's curling up on me too much." He pointed to a couple of spots of shiny scar tissue. "I think if I get these cut back I'll have a better range of movement. I may need to get a skin graft if it won't release correctly. I'll talk to the plastic surgeon and see what can be done."

He flexed the hand in front of her and she could see what he meant. Over time the burn scars had thickened, but when they thickened they tightened and pulled tight, in the only direction it could— that of the bend of the wrist. Lora thought about when she had first met Chad, he had had a stronger range of movement then.

Once again, things were happening in her family and she'd been oblivious. How long had he been thinking about this? It was obvious that it had been bothering him recently, otherwise he wouldn't have brought it up.

Cupping her hand beneath his own, she ran the fingers of her opposite hand over the puckered skin. This had never repelled her. Neither had the marks on his neck. It only made her heart ache for him.

"We'll do what we need to do to get you fixed up. You know that."

One side of his mouth tipped up. "I know, darlin'." He tipped his chin toward Mercy, whose head was now hanging off the bench. "Think she's comfortable like that?"

Wincing, Lora shook her head. "I doubt it."

Pushing to his feet Chad crossed the room to the little

girl. Whispering to her softly he lifted her head to the horizontal and repositioned Lora's purse beneath her. Mercy smiled slightly and hummed something. Chad pressed a kiss to her forehead and returned to his seat, kicking his booted feet out in front of him.

Lora wished hospitals would be more considerate of their waiting families, because these chairs were not made for sitting for any length of time.

Her phone buzzed in her pocket, nagging at her. Chad plopped his hat over his face and leaned his head back against the wall, folding his arms across his broad chest. "Go do what you need to do, babe. I'm going to catch a few winks."

Leaning over she pressed a kiss to his neck. He hadn't shaved for a while and dark stubble was growing in, but it only made him that much sexier to her. "I'll be back in a while. Can I have the truck keys? I might go get my computer."

"They're in my pocket," he told her.

Beneath the brim of his hat she could see him grinning. Taking the dare, she reached her hand into the depths of his hip pocket, making sure to fumble around like she couldn't find them. Actually, she didn't find them. Just a few wrapped mints.

"Oh, sorry," he murmured. "Other side."

Lora heard the laughter in his voice and she laughed. "You are so bad," she hissed.

"Hey, I have to get what I can get these days."

She moved around him and burrowed into his second hip pocket. The keys were there, but she took her time, first stroking his thigh, then the hardness she could feel growing beyond her fingers.

"I'm tired, baby, but not that tired. Want me to join you in the truck?"

Lora knew she was blushing at the thought, but it also excited her. "No," she laughed, but it didn't sound very firm.

They had escaped for a date on a beautiful night. Chad took her on a picnic on a mountaintop. It had been panoramic and beautiful, and they had made love beneath the stars. That was the most daring place she'd ever made love. But the thought of straddling him in the driver's seat of the blacked-out truck suddenly held more appeal than it ever had before. "If we weren't at a busy hospital for your sick father, with Mercy mere feet away, I would think about it," she admitted.

He pushed the hat up on his head, looking at her fully. His eyes had gone dark with arousal and Lora shivered. She knew that look. It meant long, slow, delicious delights she'd grown to love. Chad had taught her things about making love and her own body that she could never have dreamed of. He'd brought her out of her previous life better than she'd ever been.

She smiled at him, promising him silently that she would cash in on his offer, just not now. With a sexy wink, he tipped his head back against the wall. "Love ya, babe. You know where we'll be."

Lora hated to leave them, the two most precious pieces of her heart. But if she sacrificed some time now, she would be able to be with them later when they were awake. On the way down to the truck she detoured to the cafeteria and grabbed a coffee. It was surprisingly good, and eased the chill of the early morning from her bones. The truck seemed comfortable enough, and private so that she could check her email. First she emailed William to give him an update on what was going on. He returned her email almost immediately, in spite of the early hour, so she called him.

"Why are you up so early? Isn't it like four a.m. there? Do you sleep?"

"Of course I sleep, but I don't require much. Tell me what's going on."

William Sparks, Jr. was concerned about the family situation, but not overly so. Lora knew when she'd called him that she would have to set some limits for his contacting her, and he wasn't wild about the restrictions. Actually, he seemed a little put out, as if he couldn't believe she wasn't pawning the family off on other members to deal with the company she ran. "I have faith in you, William. Once things settle down here I'll try to catch a flight into the city and we can talk about things in person."

That seemed to appease him. "I'll start an agenda and I can update you when you call in."

Lora sighed. Traveling to New York was her least favorite thing in the world to do. All of the crowds and noise put her on edge and shot her anxiety through the roof. She'd only been up there twice, once with Chad and once without. If she hired a car to meet her at the airport, it usually went ok. Then they were responsible for getting her place to place.

"I want you to be clear that I'm not sure when I'll be calling in, so you have my okay to operate the company as you see fit for this period of time. And William?"

"Yes, ma'am?"

Lora thought about Mercy's new haircut, and the other things she'd noticed recently. She might need to take some real time off soon. "You're doing an excellent job. Keep doing what you're doing."

There was a long pause on the other end of the line, and she wondered how often he was complimented about anything.

"Of course, ma'am. I wish your father-in-law well."

Lora smiled slightly. He probably wished Garrett well because he didn't want to deal with her being gone longer than expected.

William was a machine in the boardroom, but she actually worried about him a little. The Malone Corporation was one of several companies he had operated or advised upon. When she'd hired him through a personal recommendation from Kendall Herrington, the wife of one of the vets Chad worked with, she'd thought he was too much of a stick in the mud. She'd realized, though, over the months, that he just didn't have a great family experience. His mother had died young and his father was a workaholic, still running a tech company somewhere out on the West Coast. During one of their New York meetings, he'd seemed a little distracted. When she'd asked him what was wrong he'd admitted that his father was trying to take over one of the companies William served on the board for. He'd seemed ... *businesslike* when he'd talked about it, but Lora wondered if it had actually hurt his feelings. Eventually, she decided he seemed disheartened, which was saying a lot for William.

But he ran the Malone Corporation as if it were his own. Stock prices were up and it was doing more business than it ever had. The new management had freshened everything, giving the stockholders and the personnel encouragement that business was progressing better than ever. There had been holdouts, of course. Some of the men on the board had been there since Rosalind herself had taken over the company from her father, many years ago. As each quarterly report rolled in though, and they saw how much work she and William were putting into the company, they'd begun to come around. There were still a few who refused to believe that Lora would be able to run the company herself, which was fine. She had at least a couple of years of classes and tutelage before she could even contemplate trying to run it herself.

Lora worked on her computer for a couple of hours in the quiet of the truck. She returned calls as she needed to, warning people that she would be out of pocket for the next few days and would return calls when she could. Most seemed understanding, but there were a few that just couldn't seem to imagine *not* doing business, no matter what was going on with the family in their lives.

Those people put her own situation into sharp contrast. She couldn't imagine not being here for Garrett and the rest of the family. Did that mean that she wasn't as invested in business as she needed to be? Surely there had to be a happy medium, where both could be accommodated?

Lora worked for a couple of hours, until she couldn't keep her eyes open any longer. Setting her phone alarm for nine, she reclined the truck seat, shoving a jacket beneath her head for a pillow. Before she drifted off she smiled to herself. Just a year ago she would never have had the confidence to sleep exposed like this. It was nice to be strong.

CHAPTER 7

When Lora walked into the waiting room the next morning, Chad was taken aback. With the way the sunlight was shining in and catching her blonde hair, she was stunning—absolutely breathtaking. She'd obviously gotten a couple hours of sleep, because she looked refreshed and focused. Mercy went over and hugged her mother, leaning against her heavily as Lora rubbed her back. Chad didn't know if Lora realized it or not, but Mercy was gaining height on her. In the past year the girl had grown inches, surely because her lifestyle had improved. She wasn't as nervous anymore, and wanted to explore the world around her. Though Lora was holding tight and not wanting Mercy to grow up, growing up was inevitable.

Cheyenne and Brock came in a few minutes later, obviously having walked in together. Chad tipped his hat at Brock, and was surprised when his older brother walked over and pulled him in for a rib-crushing hug. Then he leaned down and hugged Lora and Mercy as well. Lora glanced at Chad, her green eyes large with surprise, but he shrugged. He wasn't sure what had come over Brock. That was the first show of brotherly affection they'd had in years.

Cheyenne grinned behind his back and mouthed, 'we'll talk later'.

Chad, Brock and Cheyenne all went in to their father's hospital room together. When their mother looked up, she smiled at them, then motioned to their father.

Garrett Lowell looked like death warmed over, but he was sitting up in the bed, glowering. Mama was holding a white plastic hospital cup out toward him, straw extended. "I'm not drinking out of that sissy cup," he complained.

He looked up and gave a weak smile when he saw his kids at the end of the bed. "Well look at you three. I haven't seen you all together for years. Too bad Emily's not here. I guess I have to really be sick for her to come home."

Chad grimaced, feeling guilty. It had been a long time since they'd all been together. Christmas maybe? No, there'd been some kind of issue and they'd missed each other. He'd only seen Brock twice since the big showdown with Derek Malone, and both times had kind of been in passing. Actually, Chad thought Brock had been avoiding him. Maybe because he'd gotten together with Lora? He had no idea. That had been a while now, he thought, over a year at least. He shook his head, wondering where the time had gone.

For the first time, Garrett looked old to him, his normally bright blue eyes, so like Chad's own, shadowed. With the washed out color, and the messed up gray-black hair and no hat, he looked totally out of his element in the bright white hospital bed. Garrett had always been a good-looking man who kept up his appearance. In his youth he'd been chased by the girls, Mama had said, but he'd only ever had eyes for her. Brock and Emily took after him coloring wise, dark-haired and strong-chinned, although Brock's bright blue-green eyes were definitely a curious variation. Emily, Chad and

Cheyenne had all gotten blue eyes like their parents. Cheyenne looked the most like Mama had when she'd been a girl, with deep auburn hair and clear blue eyes. The four siblings were a bit of a mix.

Chad could tell Garrett wasn't feeling well. Pain killers had faded the sharpness of his eyes. His broken arm was twice the size it normally was, in part because of the amount of bandage binding it. But he still managed a grin at them and shake his head. "First time I've gone ass over teakettle since I was a kid," he groused.

Cheyenne stepped to the side of the bed and leaned over to give him a kiss on the cheek. She'd cleaned up and it was obvious she'd gotten some good sleep, too. Maybe not enough, but they'd all catch up eventually. "I wish I'da been there to take a picture," she teased. "You can't crow about your riding ability anymore."

"Not my fault my ticker decided to throw me out of the saddle."

Cheyenne grinned and moved back to let Chad in close. He reached out and squeezed his dad's left hand on the mattress. "You scared us, old man. Are you in any pain?"

Garrett shook his head. "They've got me on enough drugs to knock out an elephant. That's what the nurse said. But I keep coming around."

As he spoke, though, his eyes began to drift closed. Chad let his hand go and moved back so that Brock could get in beside the bed. "The babies are all taken care of and we found that heifer that had disappeared. She's got a big bull calf at her side now."

Garrett roused and grinned. "I knew she'd have a big' un."

Then his eyes fluttered shut again and he let out a light snore.

Francine laughed lightly, though she looked tired. "He keeps dozing off in the middle of conversations. Then he'll wake back up still talking. But he's doing good. The doctor was in already and says everything looks perfectly normal. As long as he continues to improve they'll schedule his arm surgery for two days from now."

"Then it's a good time for you to get out of here for a while," Cheyenne told their mother firmly.

Francine opened her mouth to object but Cheyenne cut her off. "No, Mama. You've been in this same spot for almost two days. You need to get out of here and get some sleep. Take a shower. Eat a decent meal. The hotel room is right across the street."

Frowning, Francine looked at her husband. "I don't know," she murmured.

"We do know," Chad told her. "You need to get sleep now while he's kind of out of it, because he's going to be giving these nurses fits when they actually let him wake up."

She smiled, then chuckled. "Yes, he will. I don't know how we're going to slow him down. He's so used to working all the time he barely even finds time to eat."

"And you do the same thing, Mama," Brock told her smoothly. "Go relax for a few hours. Cheyenne and I will stay here while you, Chad, Lora and Mercy go back to the hotel and take some time for yourselves."

Her eyes brightened at the mention of Mercy's name. "Maybe I will do that. But you call me if anything changes, Brock Ian Lowell."

"Yes, ma'am." Brock tipped his black hat to her in promise, his eyes twinkling with humor.

Francine gathered up her things, then with a final kiss to her sleeping husband's forehead, left the room. Mercy squealed when she saw her grandmother, and raced in for a hug. Francine laughed, rocking her back and forth in her arms. "You're too big for me to pick up now," she complained. "I used to be able to carry you."

"I'm *eight* now, Grandma! I'm way too old to be carried like a baby."

Lora leaned in for a hug as well, murmuring softly to Francine. They shared nods and turned to Chad. "I'm ready, Chad. Cheyenne gave me the key card thing, so let's go. I'll maybe eat something and get some sleep, then I'll come back in a few hours."

Chad nodded and they trooped to the truck. The hotel was still serving a breakfast so they ate there. Chad could tell his mother was tired, because she was so much quieter than normal. Any other time she would have been digging into what they'd been doing over the past several months, since they'd last visited. His mother called all the time, but it wasn't the same as actually being together and catching up.

If she wasn't worried about her husband and about to keel over from exhaustion, she would have been her usual irrepressible self. There wasn't much in this world that could keep Francine Lowell down for long.

Cheyenne texted him while they were eating.

Payton talked to Brock last night on the phone. Reminded him that none of us were going to live forever. Might be why he was almost personable this morning.

Huh. That was interesting.

Ok, thanks for letting me know, Sis. Love ya!

Love you too, lil bro.

When they finally went to their rooms, they all heaved sighs of relief. It had been a long couple of days. Mercy seemed thrilled that she would have her own bedroom. In no time she had stripped down to her t-shirt and panties and bounced into the bed, flicking the TV on with the remote. Arms behind her head, she settled down smack in the pile of pillows to chill.

Chad headed for the shower in the other bedroom. He

was grimy as hell. His stump felt chafed and he needed to stretch out. And his back was killing him for some reason.

All of that went out of his head, though, when he walked into the bathroom and found Lora in her bra and panties. Surprised, he gave her a smile. Normally when she met him in the shower it meant she wanted loving. "I got you excited talking about making love in the truck, didn't I?"

Her fair skin flushed as she turned to him. "Maybe a little. Is Mercy occupied?"

Chad nodded. "Watching Dogs 101 on Animal Planet. She'll be asleep in no time, even though it's," he screwed his eyes up toward the ceiling, "ten o'clock in the morning?"

"She didn't sleep well on that bench. She'll burrow into the covers and take a nap."

Chad nodded, agreeing, already planning on locking the door as soon as they got out of the shower. And maybe they'd leave the shower running cold to mask the noises they were going to make. He looked at the floor. Hell, maybe they'd make love right here. No, that was gross. He was getting hard and hungry though. It had been at least a couple weeks since they'd made love.

"Wanna shower first?"

She nodded, reaching behind her back for the clasp of her white bra.

Chad stared at her, proud of how she'd grown as a woman. When they'd first gotten together, the lights had to be off when they made love, and she'd rarely instigated. She'd gone to counseling to get over the sexual abuse her ex had put her through, but it had still been a long healing process. Chad had swallowed down everything he'd needed in order for her to grow. It had taken months before she'd allowed him to make love to her in the daylight. Showers together were few and far between. But as she'd gotten more comfortable with him, knowing that he loved her no matter what her issues, they'd begun to ease. Then she'd gone into a phase when she'd blushed when they'd talked about sex, and it had been charming and thrilling to him, because she was finding joy in the mere thought of making love. Then one night she'd walked into the bedroom naked, pushed him back onto the mattress and ridden him like he'd never been ridden before. It had been the beginning of an incredible phase in their love life.

Then work and school had begun to intrude more and more. It seemed like such a lame excuse, but there it was. After working ten or twelve hour days, running Mercy around, cooking, taking care of the house and whatever issues popped up, it had been a lot to make the effort to make love. Lora had been run just as ragged this year, between trying to get her degree in business and actually running the Malone Corporation.

William was still shouldering the bulk of the work but he was taking Lora's input more and more. Chad had a feeling that if they didn't come to some kind of understanding soon he was going to lose the little bit of time she gave them now.

As stressful as the past two days had been, he was heartened by her response. She was doing and saying everything a significant other should when a loved one was in the hospital, and it reminded him again of what a genuinely kind person she was. Mercy was going to have the same kind of personality, although he could already see sparks of rebellion in the girl. No, not rebellion, he thought. Independence.

Lora stood naked before him now, her head cocked to the side and a smile tilting her lips. She knew what she did to him and she loved that power.

"You are beautiful," he told her softly. "Even after hours of discomfort and in a hard situation, you shine. I love that about you. And you were so considerate with my mom."

Her smile broadened. "I think you might be overtired. I didn't do that much. Besides, she's my mom, too."

Yes, she was. Francine had taken Lora under her wing as much as Lora would allow on their visits, especially when she learned that Lora's mother had passed a few years ago from cancer. And as much as Lora wanted to guard herself, Francine, in her own steam-rollerish way, was charming.

Lora moved toward him and his mind shifted gears. Reaching out, she started unsnapping his blue plaid shirt. Chad tracked the progress of her nimble fingers down till they hit his belt buckle. She maneuvered his hips like a pro as she tugged and popped the mechanism free, then did the same to the button and zipper of his jeans. Then, stepping even closer, and with a devilish look in her eyes, she ran her hands from his hips and around to cup his butt cheeks, pushing the fabric away as she did. With a quick bend she pushed them all the way down to his ankles. She waited while he stepped out of the clothing, then tossed it aside.

Chad loved the look in her eyes when she looked at his bobbing erection. When she took his dick in her hand, he sighed appreciatively. "That feels incredible. I have to admit, he and I, we're pretty hungry."

Lora looked up at him and lifted one brow. "I am too, actually. In fact, I was thinking," she looked at the counter-top, "that this would be about hip height to you."

Chad tightened his jaw as he looked at the bathroom counter. She *had* been thinking about it. All of their personal grooming items had been placed on one side of the counter, and the other side had been covered by a towel. Yeah, her butt would get cold on the stone, he thought with a smile. "Hm. Let's see."

Without giving her a chance to move, he picked her up and set her on the edge of the counter, spreading her legs around his hips. She gasped as she looked down to where they met.

Yes, it was the perfect height, and her mouth was within easy reach too. Cupping her head in his hand he pulled her to him. Angling his head, he kissed her hard. With a moan she leaned into him, resting her hand on his jaw. Chad wished he had shaved for her beforehand because her skin blemished easily. He would just try to be gentle.

Lora didn't seem to be worried about the feel though. She was too lost in the moment. When she shifted against him and reached between them to angle him in, he let her. Then he guided her knees up around his hips as he pushed into her.

"Oh, Chad," she sighed.

Her perfect breasts with their hard pink nipples pressed against his chest. He looked down the slim line of her tummy and to the nest of pale blond hair below. It mingled with his own much darker hair. Drawing his hips back, he watched his body pull out of hers. His aching dick glistened with wetness. That was all her. For a moment he stilled, just feeling the throb of his pulse strum into his sex, and into her heat. His heart raced as he pushed forward again, going deeper than he had the first time. She exhaled in time with his movement, moving her arms to wrap around his shoulders and neck. He felt her heels dig into his flanks and he knew she could come this way. She'd already begun to quiver.

Chad looked up into the mirror behind her and was struck with the eroticism of the moment. Lora was significantly smaller than he was, but she was strong. The long muscles along the length of her spine flexed as she arched into his thrusts. Her perfect little ass was dimpled by his fingers. He flexed them into her flesh just to see it, and she panted into his neck. Still holding her ass he pulled his hips back, then slammed forward again, and again. Leaning his head down he nibbled at the tender skin of her neck, just like she was doing to him. He glanced up at the mirror, watching himself curl into her, his arousal burning.

She broke first, her head tilting back as her pleasure began to overwhelm her. Shifting his hold, Chad spread the fingers of his right hand over the base of her spine, pulling her in tight against him. With his weaker left hand he tugged at her distended nipples. Lora cried out, one arm bending behind her head, lifting her breast higher for his attention. Chad could feel her body twitching, jerking as she neared the crest and he shifted his touch to her other breast even as he leaned down to scrape his teeth along her earlobe. Tightening his fingers, he tugged on her breast, his body grinding into hers. He felt her pussy clamp down until he could hardly move, then suddenly ripple as her orgasm rolled over her. Crying out, she dug her fingernails into his shoulders, her body jerking in his hold. Chad's vision had gone dark, though, as his pleasure responded to hers. The rolling contractions of her body's pleasure brought his own. He tipped his own head back with a growl, gripped her hips in his hands and pushed into her as hard as he could.

The pleasure rolled through him hard, arching his back and tightening his muscles, but even as he came he had to be cognizant enough to keep his feet. He held Lora to him as tightly as he could without bruising her, his release filling her.

"Oh, damn," he moaned, struggling to keep his quivering thighs braced as his orgasm receded. Eventually a wave of relaxation hit him, then it was really hard to keep his feet. Chad looked down into her shining eyes and smiled. "I needed that," he admitted.

One side of her swollen mouth kicked up. "You know, I did too."

Feeling like a voyeur, he looked down their bodies again as he backed away from her. What a beautiful sight she was as she put her knees together and slipped from the vanity. She padded to the shower and turned it on. Within seconds the hot water was rolling steam through the small bathroom.

Chad wanted to lose himself in the love he felt for Lora. He'd gotten a little guarded about expressing himself and what he wanted, because he wanted her to follow her dreams, he truly did, even if he was inconvenienced a little. It wasn't fair for him to put his needs ahead of her own. But, he had been disappointed when he had expressed some minor wish, only to be shut down by her schedule.

Pushing all that bitterness away, he reached for the shower gel. He would enjoy this moment for as long as he could.

CHAPTER 8

GARRETT HAD a scowl on his face like she'd never seen before. He sat straight up in the bed, scowling at the nurse that puttered around him. "What do you mean it's been delayed?"

The woman smiled at them, calm, and shrugged her shoulders slightly. "The surgeon has had two emergencies one right on top of another. Your surgery has been delayed."

"Mine is an emergency, too," Garrett growled.

The woman's smile never wavered as she tapped something into a tablet. "Technically it's not. You are stable at this moment. Mr. Lowell," she told him chidingly, "do you really want a surgeon who's been up for twenty-eight hours to operate on you?"

Garrett frowned and looked to Francine. Chad's mother shrugged lightly. "She's right, dear. You don't want him to mess this up. It's too important."

Scowling, he looked out the window beyond her head. "I need to get home," he complained. "I can't be sitting here on my ass while the ranch goes to hell."

Chad shared a glance with Lora, then looked back at his father. "Dad, you know it's not going to hell. Brock and

Jackson are taking care of everything. They wouldn't let the Blue Star decline in any way."

Garrett continued to glower and Lora wondered what he needed to hear. Francine seemed to be at a loss too. She rubbed her husband's good hand.

Lora stepped forward to the end of his bed. "What do you need right now, Garrett? How can we make you feel better about being here?"

He shook his head mutely and he reminded her so much of Chad in that moment, stubbornly clamping his lips and not letting anyone in. "I'm tired," he said finally. "I want a nap. And I want something to eat. If he's not going to operate I need some food."

The nurse smiled her standard smile. "I'll order you a tray, Mr. Lowell."

Reaching for the side rail he pushed the button to lower the head of the bed.

"Okay, we'll let you take a nap. We're going to take Francine down to eat something. We'll be back in a little bit."

He didn't acknowledge them as they left the room.

Francine allowed Lora to wrap her arm around her shoulders. "He's just frustrated and not feeling like himself at all," she told her.

"I know," Lora told her softly. "And I don't blame him. He's had a lot to deal with in the past few days. You have too. But you're both doing very well."

Chad reached out to rub his mother's back and she leaned into him for a hug. "Let's grab Mercy and we'll go get some lunch."

~

IF ANYTHING, Garrett was worse when they returned. Resorting to guerrilla warfare to improve his mood, they

63

snuck Mercy into the room. Her eyes widened when she saw Garrett in the hospital bed but she didn't freak out. Lora had worried that seeing him like that would scare her, but her little girl tipped up her chin and marched to the side of the bed. "Hey, Grampa."

Garrett gave her a smile. "Hey, Munchkin. Got a smooch for your old pap?"

Mercy climbed to her knees on his good side and leaned into him to give him a kiss.

Garrett's mood did improve with Mercy's visit, but he still seemed so restless. When she murmured that to Chad, he nodded. "He's used to doing literally everything. It's like when Duncan needed his surgery. He had to let go of a bit of the control and it was a lot harder than he thought it would be. Dad's been in control of the ranch much longer than Duncan, though. The better part of thirty-five years, anyway, when he took over from his father."

Lora nodded, wrapping her arm through his as they sat in the chairs and watched Mercy play checkers with Garrett on the rolling bedside table. Before long, though, Garrett was looking tired.

"We should let him sleep," Lora suggested.

Chad nodded. "Dad, we're going to go out and let you sleep. Might take my girls around Amarillo and let them look around. See if we can catch a tiger or something."

He waved a hand at them but didn't say anything. He did lean over for Mercy to give him a kiss on the cheek and gave her a wink in return.

"Mama, do you need anything?"

Francine shook her head. "No, I'm good. Cheyenne packed everything I needed. And I have a book and games on my phone for when he's sleeping."

They headed out of the hospital and Lora was shocked at how bright everything was. They'd been in the hospital all morning waiting for Garrett's surgery. Now that it was cancelled till the next day they had some free time on their hands.

Chad led them to the truck and they climbed in. He swatted Mercy on the butt as she got in and she giggled.

Lora loved hearing her laugh. Sometimes the sound caught her off guard and she moved to quiet her before she remembered that Derek wasn't around any more. It was just habit to curb the noise.

"Mind if we go to the zoo?" Chad asked them. "It's not very big but they have a nice variety of animals."

"That sounds wonderful."

"Yes, yes, yes!" Mercy chanted.

Chad drove them to the zoo and they spent a leisurely couple of hours there. Mercy loved the ring-tailed lemurs and their crazy antics.

"When I brought Grace, Caroline and Savannah a couple years ago they loved them, too," Chad told her.

She also seemed entranced by the lions, thought they weren't particularly active. In the heat of the day they lay beneath the shade of a rock overhang in their enclosure, tails lazily swatting flies.

"They're just like the horses, swatting with their tails," Chad laughed.

Mercy giggled, reaching for his hand.

Lora watched the interaction, a little shocked that this kind of happiness had wandered into her life.

After touring for about an hour they hit a thatched hut ice cream stand. Chad guzzled a bottle of water, the muscles in his throat rippling as he swallowed. He wore a Grunt Style muscle shirt with a stylized skull on the front, shaded with the colors of the American flag. The ever-present Levis and Ariat cowboy boots clad his bottom half. Today he wore a ball cap instead of his Stetson, and he looked scrumptious, his lean muscles bulging as he played with Mercy. They'd made love this morning in the bathroom but she could feel her body hum with excitement as she looked at him.

"You're husband is very good looking."

Lora startled a little and jerked her head to look at the woman speaking. She was an older woman and seemed to just be holding a table. Her family must be in line for ice cream.

"Thank you very much," Lora murmured. She didn't correct her on the husband part. "I think so, too."

"And your daughter is a beautiful mix of you both."

Again, she didn't correct the woman's assumptions, just nodded her head. "Thank you so much."

"No, thank you for taking the time to be with your daughter." She waved a hand at the line. An older man and two boys stood in line, looking up at the sign and trying to decide what to order. "We bring our grandsons here, and we love spending time with them, don't get me wrong, but I wish my daughter and her husband would take the time from their schedules to do this sort of thing from time to time. They work too hard."

Lora nodded. "It's easy to fall into that trap."

She was saved from more conversation as the woman's family returned. Finishing their cones, Mercy and Chad stood to throw their trash away. With a final wave at the friendly woman, Lora followed them.

It *was* easy to fall into the never-ending work trap. For the past year and a bit she'd done almost exactly that. In her mind she kept telling herself she was doing it to secure Mercy's future, but that wasn't completely the truth. There was a lot of satisfaction in having input in the running of the huge investment corporation. She could see the immediate effect of her actions on the response of the personnel and especially on the movement of the stock market. It was a true gauge to what had been happening with the company. When Rosalind Malone had been murdered the stock had plunged, then plunged even further when Derek exposed for what kind of man he was and how much money he had embezzled from investors. It had been an incredibly hard road bringing the failing company back from ruin. And it had taken a lot of very intelligent, savvy business people to help her do that.

Now the company was back in the black. The stock was climbing and they were being innovative, looking for ways to grow. Rosalind had been content with the status quo, but Lora would not be. She couldn't be. Not anymore.

Chad reached for her hand. Curling her fingers around his, she swung their hands together. The sun was sliding down the sky, but the past few hours had been idyllic. It seemed like an ideal time to talk to him about a few things, though she felt a little nervous.

"I want to tell you that I'm sorry I've been working so hard recently," she told him. "I think I've gotten a little blind to everything going on around me. Without sounding like I'm making excuses, learning to run this business has been beyond difficult. Even with William's help. And there are certain things I'll never learn, probably." She paused and turned to him. Mercy had stopped at the bear exhibit and seemed absorbed. "But I want you to know that I see everything you've done to keep our family running, and I love you for it. Well, I love you for many things, but that's one of the biggies right now. The other biggie is how much you love Mercy. You are the father she's always deserved to have, I was just unable to give her."

Chad lifted his sunglasses to the top of his hat. "You shouldn't take responsibility for anything to do with Derek. He saw a vulnerable young woman, whose mother had just died, and he took advantage. He wanted a pretty piece of arm candy and you fit the bill." He reached up and caught some hair the wind was trying to steal, tucking it behind her ear.

She laughed. "Right. I don't know about the arm candy bit but I'll try not to feel guilty."

Chad shook his head, his bright blue eyes direct. "You're a beautiful woman, Lora, and you rock my world. I can't tell you that enough. I know you've been working your ass off and I'm proud of everything that you've accomplished."

Lora's eyes burned with tears and she had to look away from the directness of his stare to take a breath. But she had to look at him again, because everything he said was right there for her to read in his expression. She knew in her heart he loved her. It was just hard for her to feel worthy of it.

"Thank you, babe. As much as I hate that your father is having issues I appreciate the chance it's given me to take a bit of a break," she laughed. "It's been a long time since we did something like this."

Chad wrapped his arm around her shoulders and pulled her tight against him. Lora buried her nose into his neck and inhaled, loving everything about him. He had a scent to him that was pure masculinity but it was tempered by sweetness, usually because he had some kind of candy either in his mouth or in his pockets. It had become Chad's scent.

He stroked his hand down her back. "I know this has thrown your schedule out of whack."

She shrugged against him. "I emailed my professors to let them know. They're flexible. And William knows what's going on. We do most of our business by phone and email anyway."

"I'm not sure what's going to go on with Dad, but I want to be available if Mama or Brock needs me."

"Of course," she leaned to look up into his face. "Do you think they'll need help on the ranch?"

He pulled in a heavy breath. "I'm not sure. It kind of

sounds like it. I guess I'll have to talk to Brock about it and see what he says. I have no idea how long the recovery time will be. And I don't think he'll bounce back a hundred percent."

She nodded. So much was up in the air right now.

They left the zoo a bit later and headed out to get some dinner, but on the way back to the hospital for a final Garrett check Mercy fell asleep in the back of the truck. Rather than wake her and drag her through the hospital to wait in the waiting room they decided to take her to the hotel, and Lora would stay with her.

"If you need anything call me," she told him firmly.

He pressed a kiss to her lips. "I'll be back in a bit."

A few hours later he climbed into bed and pulled her tight against him. "Everything is good," he assured her. "Go back to sleep."

CHAPTER 9

THE SURGERY WENT SURPRISINGLY FAST the next day. Actually, it took a couple of hours, but that was a small amount of time compared to what they had already waited.

The doctor, a disturbingly young man with kind eyes, came to the waiting room with a smile on his face. He headed straight for Francine.

"Your husband will be fine."

Mama nodded her head, as if she'd had no doubt. Chad reached out to rub her shoulder and she gave him a vague smile. Cheyenne had her arm wrapped around her shoulders and Brock stood leaning against the wall. Emily, who he hadn't seen for months, had walked in just a few moments ago, and now stood with her arms crossed over her stomach. Lora had met the young woman for the first time just a few months ago and she could tell she was no-nonsense and incredibly smart. Chad had called her Brainiac and pulled her in for a tight, brotherly hug when he saw her.

"The fracture went together easily once I got in there," the doctor told them. "But it was a proximal humerus fracture, meaning that the ball of the humerus had broken off, as well as the break in the humerus bone itself. He has a long plate going up the length of the bone and eight screws to fix the three pieces together. I'm hoping this will be the end of the repair, but these kinds of injuries are difficult sometimes. It's very common for patients not to regain full use of the arm even with extensive physical therapy, which he will require."

Chad cringed. PT was a necessary evil. Dad would not be happy.

"The good news is that the radial nerve seems fine. We'll check with Garrett in a bit but I think the numbness he was feeling in that hand will be gone now."

Chad shared a look with Lora. He hadn't been aware there was numbness and it didn't look like she had either.

"When can he get out of here, Doc?" Brock asked.

The young doctor glanced up at the scowl on Brock's face then away, as if he didn't like the look. "Probably within a couple of days as long as he keeps improving. He's going to be on a movement restriction, though. These fractures are notoriously bad about not healing well."

The doctor grinned and shook Francine's hand. "If there's anything you need my number will be in the release paperwork."

"Thank you, Doctor."

He turned and walked out of the room.

For a moment they all looked at each other.

"He's not going to like the therapy," Chad warned. "He'll be stomping' and hissin'."

Lora looked at him in surprise. "Garrett will?"

Brock barked out a laugh. "Oh, yeah. You've never seen Dad when he's angry or frustrated. It's not for the faint of heart."

All of the siblings nodded their heads.

"It takes him a while to get angry," Francine added. "But when he does, the entire ranch knows it."

Chad could tell by the look on her face that Lora was surprised. "He just gets... *grumpy* when things don't go his way."

Cheyenne snorted and Emily murmured, "That's one way to put it."

"Now that he's out of surgery I'm heading back," Brock told them. "I've got a massive amount of work to do. Keep me updated, Mama."

Brock leaned into his mother for a kiss on the cheek and pulled away. He looked at Cheyenne. "Can you get her home?"

Cheyenne nodded. "Of course."

With a tip of his head Brock left the waiting room. With a look at Lora he followed his brother, but didn't catch him until he had to stop to wait for the lumbering elevator.

"Hey, Brock."

His brother looked at him from beneath the brim of his black hat, impatient. "Yeah?"

"I know it's spring round-up. Need another set of hands? Or maybe just one good one?" Chad held up his good strong hand and wiggled the fingers.

Brock propped his hands on his hips. "Don't you have a regular job to get back to?"

Chad shrugged. "I have a bit of flexibility in a situation like this. The rest of the guys will cover for me if I'm more needed here."

Brock pinched the bridge of his nose before nodding, reluctantly. The elevator door dinged and slid open. Brock reached his long arm out to hold it. "I do. I have to admit it's hell without Dad, and even without Mama to provide occasional meals. That's just one more thing the men have to do themselves. If you can get time off, I'll absolutely use you."

Chad grinned, his gut warming with appreciation. He and Brock hadn't always gotten along, but they were family. If the ranch needed something they would pull together to do it. "I'm a partner in LNF," Chad told him. "I can get time off. As soon as I can I'll be out. I think Lora and Mercy will go back to Denver."

"Well, you better be ready to work."

Then he stepped onto the elevator.

Chad laughed lightly to himself, wondering what he'd just gotten himself into. He and Brock working together could be very bad, or very good. He was hoping for good this time around.

∽

CHAD'S earlier words proved so very true. Once Garrett woke from the surgery, he was a bear. Lora only saw him a few minutes before Chad pulled her aside and walked her to the waiting room.

"Brock told me he needs help at the ranch, so we need to think about some things. Are you okay driving back to Denver alone?"

She frowned at him. "Why on earth would I do that?"

He looked confused, tipping his ball cap back on his head. "Well, I didn't think you'd want to stay down here. I'm not sure how long I'm going to stay. It might be a few days or a week, maybe two weeks, as long as they need me." He made a motion to the hallways around them. "This couldn't have happened at a worse time. The calves need brought in from the pastures now to be inoculated and cut. Branded. Some of the older cows need to be culled and readied for shipment to the stockyards. It's one of the most hectic times on the ranch and it's been planned for weeks, I'm sure. We have to schedule the time so that neighbors can help."

Lora crossed her arms, thinking about the logistics of

what she had going on. "So, do you want me to stay or go home?"

Chad looked surprised. "There's no question— I want you with me, of course. I love you, any time I spend with you is good time. But I don't want to put you out any more than you already have been because of my family. You didn't sign on to be a rancher's wi- uh, fiancée."

She let the flub pass. "No, but I'm here for you. And I'm here for the family. I don't retreat to my cave when the going gets rough. I'll talk to my professors and I can talk to William from here just as easily as Denver. I'll call Heather and have her go over and water the plants and stuff. Mercy's almost on summer break anyway, so I can email her teachers and see if there's anything mandatory she has to be there for, but I think they'll just let her go when they hear the extenuating circumstances."

A soft look entered his bright eyes. "I would love to have you there, and I think it would be fun to show Mercy how I grew up. Visits are one thing, but actually working gives you a completely different perspective."

Lora laughed. "I have a feeling she's going to be all over the ranch. More than she normally is. Better tell Jackson he's going to have a shadow again."

"But it's safer than in the city," he told her. "It will be family and friends helping with the roundup. And Jackson won't mind. He loves Mercy. Everyone on the ranch does, and they'll watch out for her. I'm not sure how far along they are on the drive but it may require me sleeping out a couple nights."

She frowned, trying not to be upset by that. Even as they'd passed in the night he'd been home. Close by. "I can deal with it," she promised.

He gave her a smile that totally made her heart stutter. "I know you can, baby. I never had a doubt."

"And besides, your mother will probably need help when your dad comes home. And I assume they need food for the round-up?"

He cocked his head. "You would help her with Dad? That's really something. And yes, they always need food for the round-up workers. Many times the wives of the men working it pull the meals together. But there is usually an expectation that the host family supplies the meat."

She nodded. "That makes sense. It's not fair to the people helping to be put out financially."

Chad seemed a little overwhelmed by her willingness to help out, and she was definitely overwhelmed. There was a need for people to pitch in, though, and she would do her part.

It would definitely take some schedule finagling. She was supposed to go to New York in two weeks for a board meeting, but William could stand in for her. Her business classes were almost done for the summer. She had a paper due for one class and a pretty big test for the other. Well, if they weren't willing to work with her maybe she could get an extension to the next quarter or something.

Mercy's homeroom teacher's number was in her phone and her email on the laptop. She would call her later on today to get Mercy's absence from school straightened out.

Lora cringed as she thought about what they had brought with them. A few changes of clothes. That was it. She hadn't expected to stay in Texas very long.

"What's wrong?"

"Um, we're not really packed for life on the ranch. I didn't expect to go out there. I'm going to need some things."

Chad nodded. "Maybe Cheyenne can run you around? She knows Amarillo pretty well. I'm going to go ahead and go out. It'll take me a while to get back into the hang of things, too."

Lora nodded, her heart thudding with excitement. Or was it anxiety? Probably both.

"Okay. I love you," she told him firmly. "Go do what you need to do."

"Let's make sure Cheyenne can do all this. I'm not sure what Emily is going to do."

Cheyenne seemed surprised then delighted with the plan. "Of course I can take you shopping. We'll do that on the way out. I think Emily is going to meet us out there. She took a week off to help as well and has a rental. We might just pull all this off," she laughed.

Lora wished she had some of her enthusiasm, but she nodded anyway.

Chad said his goodbyes to his mother and Mercy. She wrapped her little arms around his neck and gave him a hound dog look, complete with sad puppy eyes. "Why do I have to go shopping? Why can't I go with you?"

Chad laughed and knelt on the floor in front of her. "Well, darlin', I'm gonna have to work as soon as I get there. It's going to be a tough, dirty job, and until you learn to ride a little better you're going to have to stick close to the ranch and your mother. When we get the cattle into the lots you can come out and help. That's where Cheyenne's girls will come out to help as well."

Mercy pouted, but nodded her head. "Okay. I love you."

She gave him the biggest hug she could, and he reciprocated, tucking a couple of packs of Smarties into her pants pocket. Mercy grinned and bopped the bill of his cap, making him mock growl at her.

Then it was Lora's turn. Looping her arms around his neck she held him tight for a long minute, kissing the side of his neck. "Be careful out there."

"You know I will, baby," he leaned back to grin at her, his white teeth flashing. Leaning down, he kissed her well enough that she wanted to head back to the hotel, but he pulled away with an even bigger grin. "I'll probably see you tonight."

∼

GARRETT WAS out of it most of the morning, so the three of them took off by noon. Lora hugged Francine tight before she left, promising to do what she could when she got to the ranch.

"I'm going to stay a few more hours until he rouses completely, then I'll drive out."

"I'll wait here and drive her out when she's ready," Emily told them. "Or maybe catch a ride with Cheyenne when they release Daddy."

Cheyenne hugged her sister tight. "I'm so glad to see you. I hate that it took Daddy being sick for us to see you. I've missed you squirt."

Emily's pale blue eyes shimmered with tears but she gave her sister a smile. "I've missed you too, Trouble."

Cheyenne laughed. "Seems like you were the trouble one."

Emily shook her head adamantly. "You know I wasn't. It was always you."

Giggling, Cheyenne nodded. "You may be right about that. Love ya, little chicken."

"Love you too."

"Don't hide out here too long," Cheyenne warned. "I bet Jackson would like to see you, too."

Emily's chin jerked up and her smile suddenly looked forced. But she nodded. "We'll see."

Then Cheyenne turned and guided them out of the hospital. They headed to the hotel to check Lora and Mercy out. It only took them a few minutes to pack their bags, and they were on the go again, the bags stored in the back of

Cheyenne's pretty gray Jeep Grand Cherokee. She drove them to a shopping area that seemed to have a large selection of higher end stores. Lora felt bad in thinking they were going to be in the sticks when they went to Texas. The state had the same amenities as any other state, it just had longer expanses of space between them.

"You need jeans and shirts. Did you bring enough underwear and bras?"

Lora looked at her from the corner of her eye. "Your mother has a washer and dryer doesn't she?"

"Of course, but you can always do with new bras."

Chad's energetic sister grinned and pulled into a mall. Lora cringed when she read the sign. Malls meant screaming kids and too many people, and Mercy didn't need to be subjected to that. Before she could say anything, though, Cheyenne and Mercy had both jumped out and were heading for the entrance, their clasped hands swinging between them. Lora stared at her daughter, surprised at the lack of fear.

Hurrying, grabbing her purse, she slammed her own door and jogged after them.

CHAPTER 10

THE MALL actually wasn't that crowded, but Lora was still on edge. There were too many people that insisted upon walking close to her. More than once she shifted out of the line of traffic and paused at the wall as she waited for the wave to pass. Cheyenne didn't say anything about her strange behavior, just paused and waited with her.

"Sorry," Lora muttered, feeling her skin color.

"No worries. I completely understand."

Lora looked at the other woman standing tall and beautiful and confident. She hadn't forgotten what Cheyenne had said the night they met. She'd been in an abusive relationship as well. "How- how did you get over it?"

Cheyenne's smile turned sad. "I realized that I was wallowing in my own pity and allowing him to win, and I had three little girls depending upon me. They had started to take on my fears, and I didn't want that for them. It was hard to take those first few steps but I made myself do it. The fear would have swallowed me under if I allowed it."

Lora nodded. "I feel that. It's close. Most of what I do is

indoors and solitary. When I get out into crowds like this I freeze up."

"Why?" Cheyenne asked. "What are they going to do to you? They don't know you, have no idea what you've been through or how much money you're worth. They couldn't care less about who you are. And you have just as much right to be here as they do."

Cheyenne reached out and grabbed a passing older woman. "Excuse me, ma'am. Did you know this was Lora O'Neil?"

The woman seemed a little taken aback at Cheyenne's grip, but she smiled at Lora and waved a hand. "Hi, Lora." She tugged on Cheyenne's restraining hand. "I'm sorry, Miss, but I really have to go."

Cheyenne opened her fingers and the woman merged into the flow of foot traffic.

Lora glowered at Cheyenne. "I can't believe you did that," she hissed.

Mercy covered her mouth and giggled, then moved close to hug her mother. "It's okay, Mama."

Clamping her jaw, she looked around the moving throng of people. Nobody spared them a second glance, but overcoming years of fear wasn't going to happen in an afternoon.

Taking several deep breaths she straightened her spine. "Okay, let's go."

The mall didn't have the store that she usually shopped at, but Cheyenne knew where to get good sturdy jeans and shirts for Mercy. "And you're about the same size as my Grace, so you'll be able to wear her clothes too, if you'd like. I'm sure she'd share with her cousin."

Mercy beamed at the words. "I would love to share with her. It would almost be like having a sister." She looked around the racks of clothing before her. "But maybe I could get a couple new things? I've never been in this store before."

Lora felt humbled by her daughter's easy-going excitement in their shopping trip. Here she was feeling defensive again, but no one was blaming her for anything. They had enough money in the bank to buy the mall itself, probably, but Mercy never asked for more than she received. Lora was used to a few small stores near their home. That was where she shopped for everything, but even she had to admit that they were limited. She glanced around the brightly colored racks. She'd never seen clothes like these either.

Cheyenne was more than happy to spend Lora's money and by the time they walked out of the store they'd gotten Mercy enough clothes for the next year, or until the next big growth spurt hit. But her little girl was grinning, insisting she haul the bags herself. She wore one of the new outfits and Lora could tell she felt good.

Next they went to a store with women's clothes in it.

"What are you, like a six?"

Lora's eyes widened. "No, a ten."

Cheyenne looked her up and down. "That may be the size you're wearing, but it's not the size you actually are. Try these on."

Lora took the handful of clothing. There were bright colors and sleeveless things, and even some glittery things like Mercy had gotten. "I don't know about these, Cheyenne."

"Just humor me, Lora, please. I've been wanting to do this with you for a long time."

Biting her tongue, she went into the changing room. Glancing around, she bit her lip. No escape from Cheyenne. She had to do this or the woman would never let her out.

The jeans Cheyenne had picked out had bling on the back pockets, but they fit fairly well. They were a little tight. She picked a shirt from the pile on the chair and changed into it, snapping up the pearl buttons.

Cheyenne's eyes widened when Lora walked out of the

dressing room and Mercy gasped. "Mama," she breathed, moving around her. "You look like a cowgirl."

Cheyenne circled Lora. "Yes, you do. Those jeans fit you like they were made for you."

"They're too tight," Lora complained.

Fitting three fingers into Lora's waistband just like she'd done to Mercy when she'd been trying on clothes, Cheyenne shook her head. "No, they fit you like they're supposed to," she corrected. "You have a nice body hiding under all those long sleeves and baggy khakis. Great boobs. I know Chad loves you no matter what you wear, but wouldn't you like to dress up for him sometimes?"

Lora looked down at the outfit. The jeans were feminine and pretty, but the shirt was almost just like one he had at home, blue plaid with pearl snaps; only this one was feminine with capped sleeves. Lora decided she looked very country. Chad would love to see her in this.

"Okay. I'll get it."

She also got three more pairs of jeans, five more shirts and blouses and a pretty flowered dress with a flirty hi-lo skirt. "You are such a bad influence on me," she grumbled to Cheyenne as she handed the checkout clerk her card. She still wore the last outfit she'd tried on. Cheyenne hadn't allowed her to change back into her khakis.

"No, I'm not. You love it and you know it."

"You did great, Mama," Mercy said, squeezing her hand. "That was very brave of you."

Lora was suddenly fighting away tears. She looked away for a moment to gather her control. "Thank you, baby."

The clerk had her sign a slip then handed her the receipt. Lora glanced at the bottom but forced herself not to react to the amount.

"Come on," Cheyenne told her. "We've got one more place to go."

She led them to a busy store full of lotions and shower gels and candles. Lora had brought Mercy to a store in the same chain once before and the girl had lost herself in smelling all the little votive candles on the far wall.

"Mercy, you stay here for a bit, 'kay?" Cheyenne told her. "We'll be next door getting your mom bras and panties."

"Okay." She waved but it was very distracted.

Lora dragged her feet. "I don't want to leave her here."

"We're going to be right next door, literally *next door*. We won't even be gone long enough for her to notice."

It took everything she had to walk away from Mercy. Even as they left, she craned to look over her shoulder.

Cheyenne stopped. "Lora, look at me."

Clenching her jaw, she looked at her.

"This is an excellent time to show Mercy how much trust you have in her. Your daughter is at an age when she needs to build her confidence to become a strong woman. Right?"

Lora nodded, reluctantly.

"We could be in here hours and she wouldn't even notice. Did you see all the other little girls in there?"

"No," she admitted.

"That's a very popular spot for them to hang. They have little trial sizes of hand sanitizer you can get for a dollar. It will take her a while to pick out the twenty I told her she could have."

Lora's eyes widened in surprise. "Twenty? Why does she need twenty hand sanitizers?"

Laughing, shaking her head, Cheyenne looked at her sadly. "She doesn't *need* them, but she'll *want* them."

Lora had a feeling Cheyenne was right, but that didn't make her feel any better about leaving her daughter where any man could steal her.

"Lora, look at me."

She looked up into Cheyenne's kind, bright blue eyes.

"You can't be with her twenty-four seven. You took out the main source of danger for her, right?"

She nodded.

"Then you need to let Mercy grow. She's not going to go anywhere, I swear to you."

As hard as walking on hot coals, Lora allowed Cheyenne to lead her into the next store. But when she got a glimpse of what they were selling, she almost turned around. "I don't know about this, Cheyenne."

The woman wasn't listening.

"You're what," Cheyenne fixed Lora with a considering eye, "a 36C?"

Cheyenne started flipping hangers. The bras on those hangers were everything that Lora was not—pretty, lacy, frilly. Cheyenne held a bra up in front of her. Lora almost pushed it away but it was the prettiest color of plum purple she'd ever seen. Against her better judgment she took the bra, trying to decide if it would fit her. Cheyenne shoved several more into her hands before guiding her to a dressing room. "If something doesn't fit let me know and I'll swap it out."

Unfortunately, everything did fit. Perfectly. As she looked at herself in the mirror, a peach lace confection boosting her decent-sized boobs up, she could imagine the look on Chad's face. His eyes would go to half-mast and his full lips would tilt up on one side. And he would get that look on his face that promised her naughty pleasure.

Just the thought of what he would think about these things was enough to get her excited.

When she stepped out of the dressing room, Cheyenne gave her a knowing smile. She walked forward and held up more silk and lace. "Let's find the matching panties for those bras."

Lora handed over her card more easily this time, though the bill was almost twice as much as her clothes. She'd gotten half a dozen bra and panty sets, some sexy little sleep pants, two nightgowns, a bathing suit that made her blush every time she thought about it, a silk robe and a set of hair ties.

Lora walked out of the store feeling as giddy as Mercy had earlier. And when she walked into the smell-good store and found her daughter in very nearly the same spot she'd left her, all of the tension in her belly eased. *Nothing had happened.* Derek and his mother weren't stalking her any more, trying to steal her child from her. There were no obvious dangers lurking, waiting to grab her.

For the first time in a long time she relaxed enough to wander a completely frivolous store, sniffing here and there. Mercy had picked out her twenty hand-sanitizers, and Cheyenne grabbed a bagful for her own daughters. Lora picked out two lotions and two shower gels that appealed to her and she even found Chad a bottle of spicy smelling shower gel. Oh, that would smell so good on him.

By the time they left the mall and headed for Cheyenne's truck, they were loaded down. And she was battling guilt again.

"I'm supposed to be on the ranch and feeding people."

Cheyenne snorted. "No worries about that. I told my friend Payton to throw some fajita meat together. It's easy and filling. They'll be more than happy with it. Anyway, we have one more stop, then we'll head home."

The next stop was an enormous boot store. Lora felt her mouth drop open at all of the different styles, colors and textures. There were boots with decorative stitching, there were boots with more bling than all of her jeans combined, and there were boots with absolutely no decoration on them at all. There was one set of boots with a real rattlesnake head on the toe. Those made her shudder.

"This is practical shopping," Cheyenne told them. "You need a set of boots and a hat, and you need to wear them everywhere you go outside. We have rattlesnakes all over the place out here, and the sun can be a real bitch. Put your sunscreen on and wear your hat at all times."

Mercy and Lora nodded. Their little group headed toward the kids' boots first. Mercy zeroed in on a set of dark purple boots with a jeweled design up the leg of the boot. When she tried them on and they fit almost perfectly, Mercy danced in delight. "These are the ones I want."

Lora agreed that they were perfect for her and they moved to the women's section. The sheer amount of choice was overwhelming. Lora gravitated toward the plainer ones, of course. Then a pair of dark blue boots drew her eye. She pulled the pair from the rack and looked them over. They seemed sturdy, but pretty at the same time. Lora sat on the little bench and pulled them on. They were a little snug but the leather would relax the more she wore them, Cheyenne said.

Lora nodded her head and set them on the checkout desk with Mercy's pair. They needed to pick out hats and they would be done.

Cheyenne plonked a couple of different hats on Mercy's head till one settled correctly. It was tan, had a broad brim, and looked adorable on her. "How does that feel on?"

"Good. It's nice and shaded."

That's what Lora wanted as well.

"Most of the time you have to order hats," Cheyenne told them, "to fit your head correctly. But they take time to make and we don't really have that now. You'll have to settle for an off the rack piece."

Lora found a cream straw hat, tightly woven on the brim to block the sun but vented on the crown. There was a leather thong around the band with a string of pretty blue beads hanging from it. The thong matched her boots perfectly and when she stood in front of the mirror, she looked appropriate for where they were. There were cowboys in Colorado, but on the ranch she knew *everyone* wore hats. Even in this fairly urban shopping district nearly all the men and women she saw were wearing their hats.

Mercy refused to wear anything other than her boots and hat out, so Lora joined her. It would give them a chance to start breaking them in. The boots especially would take a little time to get used to. Cheyenne grinned at the two of them and snapped a picture on her cell-phone as they walked out of the store. "Chad is not going to know what hit him when he sees his girls."

As she thought of the bag of sexy things in the back of the car, she couldn't suppress a grin. He *wouldn't* know what had hit him.

CHAPTER 11

THE NOONDAY SUN was scorching when Chad pulled his truck in front of the main barn. It seemed too hot for late spring, or was it early summer here in Texas, he wondered with a smile. Horses in the paddock to the right stood hipshot, nose to tail with other horses to keep the flies away. Chad looked out over the expanse.

The ranch hadn't changed much in his almost thirty-four years of life. Dad had added and expanded barns, but the overall layout had stayed the same. House to the West, big barn to the East, paddocks and small barns North and South. The area had a few low hills with trees but overall it was flat and grassy. The long-ago Lowells had settled into a natural depression in the landscape so water was a little easier to come by. The Blue Star's wells always produced water and it had been a blessing for many generations.

Which was a good thing. It was significantly warmer in Texas than Colorado.

At some point while they were here Chad wanted to take Mercy to the Oasis, a spring-fed pond he, his father and Brock had developed years ago. It was just a glorified, deepened pond that they'd landscaped, but it had been one of the funnest things they'd had to do while growing up. One of the trees had a massive rope swing that would drop them almost to the far side if they didn't release soon enough.

A black-hatted man cantered up on a bright black and white paint. Broadly built, the shirt strained over his chest. His long pitch-black hair was drawn back into a thick braid beneath the hat. Chad shaded his eyes as he walked toward Jackson, and held his hand out for a shake when he dismounted.

"Chad, you old bastard. What the hell are you doing here?"

Chad grinned at Jackson Windwalker, the Blue Star foreman. "Hey, Jackson. Well, believe it or not, I asked Brock if he needed help and he took me up on the offer."

Jackson jerked the black hat off his head and started fanning himself with it. "I'm sorry. Did you say Brock Lowell accepted your help?"

Chad nodded, laughing.

"This place must be going to hell and I just haven't been told..."

Jackson had been around long enough that he'd seen many crazy things happen on the ranch. He was a couple of months older than Brock. The two of them clucked back and forth like old hens, but they were the best of friends and normally saw eye to eye on the running of the ranch.

"Well, if you're here to work lets get you kitted out. We're working on the holding pens to the north and we could use some help."

"Absolutely."

Chad took a few minutes to stow his gear in the big house, change his hat and shirt and grab a couple bottles of water before he headed to the barn. His leg felt good right now, but he'd have to care for it properly as soon as he was done tonight. Being in the saddle for any length of time would take some adjustment.

Jackson gave him a bright red sorrel with a white blaze down his head and two white socks named Oakley.

"He's only three so he's not real smart yet but he has a good heart and he'll go and go. Be gentle on his mouth."

Chad nodded, understanding that Jackson wanted his touch on the reins to be gentle. It was very easy for an inexperienced rider to bruise a horse's mouth and undo months of training. It was a vote of confidence that Jackson had given the horse to him.

Chad brushed the colt thoroughly as he stood in the cross ties before heading to the massive tack room just inside the barn door, to the right. Jackson pointed out which items he needed and Chad gathered the saddle and bridle. He hefted the huge saddle up over his shoulder, holding onto the horn with his strong right hand. This was the easiest way to carry a saddle, but it left his weak hand to do the rest of the work. Chad only dropped the bridle once on the way back to the patiently waiting horse, but he had to return a second time to retrieve the thick red and black saddle pad. Talking softly, Chad moved toward the colt, showing him the pad. Jackson hadn't said exactly how much training he'd had, so he was going slow to give Oakley a chance to get used to him.

The colt let him settle the pad onto his back with no problem. He shied a little when he lifted the saddle to his back, but calmed when Chad talked to him. Removing one of the cross ties Chad spanned the headstall of the bridle across his right hand, holding the bit in his left hand. Hoping Jackson had trained this horse as well as the others he had, he clucked to the horse and pushed the bit toward his mouth. The horse lowered his head and allowed the bit, then the headstall to be fitted. Chad nodded in satisfaction as he straightened the colt's ears and forelock, then patted him on the neck. "Good job, buddy."

Jackson had disappeared, so Chad led the horse out of the barn and tied him to the wooden beam placed for that purpose just outside the door. Then he retrieved the bottles of water he'd grabbed and packed them into his saddle bags, along with a pair of leather gloves he'd nabbed from the tack room.

"Are you ready?"

Jackson had appeared from around the side of the barn, as silent as always. The man was part Native American and had the skills to prove it. Years ago it had driven Chad and his siblings crazy because if they ever did anything wrong, it was usually Jackson that had caught them.

"Yeah, I'm ready."

Testing the horse's training, he mounted him from the wrong side. He had to, because his prosthetic left leg wouldn't twist the way it needed to when he mounted. But the colt stood firm. Chad was pretty surprised. He leaned over the side and fitted his boot into the left stirrup, then patted Oakley on the neck.

They took off at an easy trot to get the horses warmed up. Chad bounced a little as he learned Oakley's gait, but as soon as they sped into a canter he limbered up. The horse was one of the best he'd ever ridden.

Brock prided himself on the quality horseflesh he bred, and he and Jackson were two of the best trainers around. The two of them together had put the Blue Star on the map for quarter horses. Their father had made Blue Star's name known for prime beef cattle, but Brock had been behind the horses' acclaim.

As Oakley settled into a rocking canter, Chad gave Jackson a thumbs up with his bad hand. The sign was a little lame, but he conveyed the gist of it. Jackson grinned and tipped his hat in acknowledgement, the length of his coal black braid bouncing along his back.

They rode for the better part of twenty minutes, up and down low hills and finally ended near a copse of trees with a windmill that promised water in their depths. There was a flatbed truck parked near them and stacks of fence panels fastened on. Brock stood unfastening the panels, getting ready to lift them to the ground with the attached hoist.

"We need to get a temporary holding pen and sorting area set up here," he motioned. "Even with help, we don't have the manpower to drive the cattle up to the Johnson place, where we normally take them, so we're setting up a temporary holding and sorting lot. It's not ideal as doing it at Johnsons' where everything is already in place, but we had to streamline."

Chad remembered that there was normally one ranch designated to be the shipping point for the cattle going to sale. To maximize workforce, all the hands from both ranches converged on one ranch for roundup, then moved cattle to the second. That way both ranches got everything done safely. He'd forgotten that it would probably be the Johnson place this year. Maybe Tara would avoid the round-up.

This year, though, with Garrett gone and the siblings running back and forth to Amarillo, the schedule had been blown to shit. Now they needed to work with what they had. A few neighbors would show up to help, but it wasn't going to be the big production it normally was.

As Brock unloaded the twelve-foot panels with the hoist, Chad and Jackson set the panels out of the way against a tree. Brock could guide them where to start building the lot itself. It was hot, dirty work, but hours later they had what they needed. There was a large sorting pen that could accommodate several hundred cattle and two smaller pens off of it, with a spot for the shipping truck to back up to it. It wasn't ideal, but it would work.

By the time they got everything set, Chad was whipped. Yes, he worked out every day, or at least every day he could, but it had been a long time since he'd done hard physical labor like this. Brock's vigilant observation had forced him to keep going, even when he should have eased up. He could feel blood seeping down his left hand and into his glove where the skin had broken, but he didn't take it off. He could care for the nagging injury when he got back to the house.

Brock's frown hadn't changed, but it had eased a bit. He seemed satisfied by what they'd done. Chad had worked his ass off, literally lifting every fence panel into place and pinning it together with the attached hinges. His back ached, the stump of his left leg ached and his bad forearm was burning but he felt good about what they'd done.

"I'll drive the truck back," Brock said. "You guys go ahead."

Chad groaned as he lifted himself onto Oakley's back. His right arm throbbed and quivered because it always took up the slack for his weak left. He settled into the saddle and wished he'd been more prepared to do this.

They rode back to the big house in silence. Chad would like to think that Jackson was hurting too, but he doubted it. He'd seen the big man hoist double the amount of panels into place he had.

Chad wondered what Lora and Mercy had gotten into. His stomach growled and he dreamed of food they'd be able to scarf down before hitting the sack. Hell, he'd be happy with a peanut butter and jelly sandwich or six at this point. His water bottles had long since been drained, then refilled at the stock pond.

Once again they settled into a nice canter to head home. Jackson had a determined look on his face, like he was hoping Christmas had arrived at the ranch while he'd been working. Chad had told him about Emily coming out to stay for a week or so while the round-up was going on and he'd gotten this dark look on his face. He'd snugged the hat on his head and kept working, though his directions had been decidedly more terse.

It was well known on the ranch that Jackson had been sweet on Emily for a long time, culminating in wild affair when she'd been in college, but she'd not been willing to be tied down to the ranch. Plus there were some hang-ups on Jackson's side about dating his best friend's kid sister. For a long time he had avoided her as much as possible, thinking that he was too old for her. Six years wasn't a huge amount, but Jackson had thought otherwise. When he had finally decided to pursue her, it had been a fiery romance. But Emily was not content with settling down like Jackson wanted. She had an incredible mind in her pretty head and she'd wanted to use it for more than ranch work.

They had made a pact, though, that if she hadn't gotten married within ten years she had to return to the ranch to marry him. It had been witnessed by Cheyenne, Chad and Payton.

"Just for curiosity's sake, has it been ten years since Emily left?"

"Yes," Jackson snapped.

Chad felt bad about digging up the past but it was obvious by Jackson's quick response that he'd been thinking about it as well.

Oakley seemed to stretch out the closer they got to the ranch and Chad let him have his head. Jackson's big paint was not a follower though. Hooves pounded and dust flew as the horses drew neck and neck. The longer-legged paint edged out the colt as they skidded into the barn lot, kicking up the dust. Chad laughed as he circled his mount, adrenalin surging through him. Though he was tired as hell, he also felt energized and vital. He hadn't done so much physical work in a long time. When he peeled off the bloody glove he might change his mind, but he'd really enjoyed today.

There was a silver Jeep Grand Cherokee parked in front of the house. A blond in ass-hugging jeans and a sleeveless blue top stood in front of the vehicle, waving away the dust he and Jackson had kicked up. Chad stared, wondering why she seemed familiar. Damn, she had a bangin' bod.

"Chad! Why did you dust me like that!"

A two by four could have knocked him out of the saddle and he would not have been more stunned. "*Lora?*"

She grinned as she walked up to him, tilting the straw hat back on her head. Propping her hands on her hips, she lifted her eyebrows at him as if to say, *Well?* Chad scrambled out of the saddle, almost falling on his ass when his left knee gave out. Staggering, he lurched toward her.

The Lora that he had known and loved had disappeared. She'd always had a great body, but she'd never wanted to show it unless it was in the privacy of their bedroom. As his gaze wandered all the way down her shirt, her jeans, to her brand spankin' new blue boots, he could only shake his head.

The color had bloomed in Lora's cheeks, but she smiled for him. "Cheyenne took me shopping."

Chad snapped his mouth shut. "You were beautiful before, don't take this the wrong way, but you are stunning right now. Those jeans ..." he shook his head, tipping his hat back on his head. "Those jeans could not fit you any better."

Reaching out he started to touch her arm, then paused long enough to jerk his right glove off. One fingertip brushed along the outside edge of her arm, feeling the softness there. "Your skin is so pale and creamy you're really going to have to watch it in the sun. You'll burn to a crisp in no time."

Lora moved toward him like she wanted a kiss, but Chad

backed away, hands held up to ward her off. "I'm pretty gross right now, baby. Let me shower first."

But she didn't listen to him, which he totally appreciated. Grabbing him by the shirt she tugged him in for a long, lingering, wet kiss.

"I'll take care of your horse tonight, Lowell. Go shower."

The rein he still held of the patient Oakley slipped through his grasp as Jackson took it from him. Chad barely spared him a glance. He was too enamored of his fiancée. There was a light in her bright green eyes that he'd never seen before, and he couldn't say exactly what it was. There was definitely excitement, but it was more than that. She enjoyed knowing that she excited him.

"Chad, look at me!"

He looked up at Mercy at the top of the porch steps. She'd gone through a similar transformation. There was a cream colored hat on her head, a smug smile on her face and she had bright purple cowgirl boots on her feet. With bling!

Chad laughed at the silly pose she made, but waved her down toward them. "You look fantastic, munchkin."

He staggered as she slammed into him, but recovered to hug her to him.

"We went shopping today to be cowgirls, but Mom got you some sexy stuff."

"Mercy!"

Chad looked up at Lora. Her cheeks were red again. "Oh, really? Like what?"

"Oh, some bras for her tatas and pretty panties. I think she got a nightgown too, but I'm not sure. It was kinda messy in the bag."

"Mercy, what did I tell you about getting into stuff when it's not yours?" Lora demanded, trying to pull away from Chad.

He tightened his grip on her hand. "It's cute," he whispered. "Don't yell at her."

"I was picking them up when the bag fell off the bed. Not my fault it was so stuffed."

Lora shook her head, looking down at the ground. Chad could see the flush in her cheeks. Tilting her chin up, he pressed a kiss to her lips. "Maybe you can give me a fashion show later."

He expected her to redden further, but instead she gave him a sexy smile. "Already planned on it."

When she pulled away that time he let her go, then he watched her ass as she swayed up the steps and into the house. Mercy took off after Jackson to see the horses.

Chad looked around, a little dazed. Cheyenne stood a few feet away, arms crossed, grinning at him. "You are so gone on her."

"Of course I am," he agreed. "And?"

"And nothing. It's cute. She wasn't going to get anything until I told her you would think she was sexy."

Chad tipped back his head and laughed. "You were totally right. I can only imagine what else she got."

Cheyenne winked and patted him on the shoulder. "You'll love it, little brother. Talked to Mama earlier. Daddy is getting out tomorrow."

"Wow," Chad said, surprised. "I really didn't expect him to get out for a few days."

"I guess he's being a pistol," Cheyenne admitted. "Giving the nurses a hard time. I can't wait until he comes home." She rolled her eyes facetiously. "Too bad I don't have the excuse of my students to get back to."

"You're about done for the summer too, though, right?"

She scowled at him. "Yes, damn it. And you know I'll be here if I'm needed. Oh, Payton will be back in a bit. She ran dinner out to the crew watching the herd. And Emily called.

She's staying with a friend from school tonight in Amarillo, then she'll ride out with me and the parents tomorrow."

Jackson was not going to be happy about that.

Circling the car, she gave him a final wave before taking off like a bat out of hell.

Cheyenne was a gem. She lived on the far side of the ranch in a small house with her three daughters, but she was over here helping out as much as possible. At least, when she wasn't teaching at the Honeywell Elementary school. Even before Dad had been hurt she'd helped Mama out cooking for the men and the like. She was more mobile than his parents, and the girls were good helpers, too.

Personally Chad thought she was trying to make it up to them for marrying the asshole she had. Wade had been a decent guy when they'd been growing up together, but he'd gone off the deep end after being gored at a rodeo. Chad thought he'd been addicted to more than painkillers when he'd beaten Cheyenne and raped her, then left her to be found in the front yard of the house they'd shared in town. It had had a devastating effect on his once friendly, outgoing sister. She acted fine with them but she was leery of other men. Some she just plain avoided, like Sheriff Sheridan Lane. In his heart, though, Chad thought maybe she avoided the big man for other reasons.

He watched her car bounce down the driveway. Maybe she was *trying* to get a ticket.

For a moment he debated going out to check on Oakley. The horses had been pretty lathered by the time they'd gotten home. Jackson would have cooled him off. And Mercy was out there too, so Jackson would be teaching her more about horsemanship. Too many people never learn that most of horsemanship takes place on the ground, not in the saddle — not on the Blue Star. Everyone who wanted to ride a horse learned how to care for horses, hot walking, grooming, feeding and mucking out stalls. Chad smiled, knowing that Mercy was having the time of her life and soaking it all in.

Feeling a little thrill run through his gut he stomped up into the house. Where had his woman gone?

For years his mother had made the cowboys come through the back mudroom and leave their dirty boots there, but she'd made an exception for him when he got the boot prosthetic. It wasn't convenient to remove it at the mudroom and bounce through the house to wherever he was going. So, Chad was the only one allowed to wear boots in the house. He tried to not make a mess, though. Maybe if he tiptoed he wouldn't leave a visible dust trail.

His parents' suite was on the bottom level and on the far end of the house. During the years they had four teenagers tripping over each other upstairs, his mother had mentioned something about a separate, private retreat, as far away from the noisy kids as possible. Dad had started work on the bedroom addition the next day. Chad thought he'd gotten too many earfuls of their music and fighting as well. Within a month of that little mention she'd had a brand new living area added onto the far side of the house. Dad had decorated it, which had taken them all off guard, but it had turned out nice. His mother had cried. A lot. And she and dad had immediately moved into that new bedroom suite, giggling like school children.

His parents had an incredible love that had lasted many years.

Tiptoeing up the stairs, Chad headed for his parents' old bedroom. It had been redecorated to house guests when they had them, and it was where his mother had requested they stay this time. Mercy was in Chad's old room. Maybe he'd stop in there later and see if she had room for everything.

For now, though, he wanted to find his fiancée.

Pushing open the bedroom door, he scanned the area.

Not in here. He heard rustling from the walk-in closet on the far side of the room, next to the bathroom, and he caught a glimpse of Lora's arm. He paused in the doorway.

Her narrow back was to him, and she was hanging a pretty yellow shirt. Beside her on the shelf was a stack of jeans, tags removed, and in the bag at her feet he could see a glimpse of lace.

"If I take a quick shower will you model for me?"

She glanced at him over her shoulder, smiling slightly. "Maybe. You'd better hurry."

He turned and disappeared into the bathroom before she could say another word. It took him a minute to get the bloody glove off his left hand. He winced as he ran it under the sink faucet. The skin had split in several places and continued to seep blood.

Chad took the quickest shower he could, scrubbing from head to toe. He scrubbed the hell out of his leg stump even though it hurt like hell, then took care of his sleeve and pros-thetic. Lora had unpacked his bag as well, it looked like. His toothbrush was in the holder next to the sink. He scrubbed his mouth and did a quick swipe of deodorant, then wrapped his left wrist in a swath of bandage and tied it off. Towel wrapped tight around his hips he hopped out to the bedroom, settling on the bed. Scooting back against the headboard, he waited, excited. Already his body was reacting, just at the mere thought of Lora in something so sexy as the lace confection he'd seen.

Lora leaned her head out of the closet, her long blond hair hanging free. There was trepidation in her expression, but excitement too. "Are you sure we have time to do this?"

Chad had no idea, but he nodded. "Jackson has Mercy and the others won't return until tomorrow, probably. We have a little while."

She disappeared back into the closet.

Chad tried to pace his breathing. Making love to Lora was unlike anything he'd ever done before. It was elemental, visceral. There was an attraction there that simply would not be curbed or dampened.

It was harder than hell waiting for her to reappear, but he made himself stay still. If she needed time he would allow her that.

When Lora did finally reappear, he lost his breath in a whoosh. She was ethereal. A classic centerfold come to life. Golden hair curled down over her shoulders and he realized suddenly how long it had gotten. She peered at him from beneath her bangs and gave him a sultry smile. "What do you think?"

"I think you're beautiful," he told her softly.

"About the underwear, silly," she laughed. "You didn't even look."

Chad glanced down. A pale yellow lace bra lifted her breasts up and out, barely covering her nipples. Actually, he could see the shadow of her areola through the fabric itself. He glanced down the long line of her lean tummy, to the tiny little scrap of lace and satin that covered the curls at her sex. Her legs looked a mile long the way she stood. He lifted his gaze. "Like I said. Beautiful, breathtaking. Glorious. Resplendent. I would change absolutely nothing about you. I love you exactly the way you are."

When she should have been beaming, a tear slipped down her cheek. Pushing up from the bed, Chad lifted a hand to her and she walked forward. He balanced on his good leg and looked down at her. "The underwear is awesome, but I love seeing that look in your eyes more than anything. That look that says you know you turn me on. That's what gets me hard."

She looked down at the towel around his hips. Reaching out she tugged and it fell to the floor. His dick sprang up against his stomach and she giggled, then sagged against him for a hug. "I love you so much, Chad. I was so lucky that you were assigned to watch us. I'm the same way, you know. I wouldn't change anything about you. Well, I'd take some of your pain away if I could." Her fingers danced over his bandaged arm, then away.

"It's all good, baby. I had fun today. It would have been too much for Jackson and Brock to do alone. I liked getting back in the saddle again."

That was an understatement. He'd *loved* it. Squinting through the dust to try to see what he was doing, feeling the surge of the horse beneath him. When they were done with the work they'd accomplished something that needed done. It fed his Texas boy soul.

"I could tell," she murmured. "I'd like to get back into the saddle again too."

Tipping back his head, he laughed. "Anything I can do to help you out with that?"

She nodded her chin toward the bed behind him. "Maybe you can let me practice on you."

Chad fell back to the bed, bouncing on the mattress. Lora followed him down and straddled his hips. When she reached behind her to take the bra off, he stopped her hands. "Leave it on and let me appreciate it."

Laughing lightly she shimmied down his legs and wrapped her fingers around his aching length.

CHAPTER 12

T<small>HEY'D JUST GOTTEN CLEANED</small> up again and semi-dressed when they heard a vehicle pull into the drive. Lora smacked Chad's hand away from her breast and finished buttoning the shirt, hurrying to the window. "It's a dirty blue truck."

"That's Payton, Cheyenne's best friend. She ran food out to the people working the herd."

Lora finished getting dressed and waited for Chad to get presentable. "I've never met her so you can introduce me."

They headed down the stairs and toward the front door. Payton was stomping up the front steps, her arms loaded with something bulky. Chad opened the door for her and stood ready to take whatever she handed over to him.

"Hey, Chad, you pretty little thing. Good to see you, sweet cheeks."

The woman with long black hair leaned up to press a kiss to his cheek. Lora felt her brows raise but didn't say anything as she waited for the woman to spot her. Instead the woman turned in the opposite direction, passed through the front entry and headed straight for the kitchen. Two giant roaster pans in her arms obstructed her view. Chad reached to take one but the woman moved away quickly. "I've got it."

Chad closed the door and they headed to the kitchen. The woman set the pans on the counter, then turned to face them.

She was stunning, Lora thought in amazement. Thick, straight black hair hung to her curvy waist. For some reason she expected brown eyes, but they were a startling, clear green. And they were the most expressive eyes she'd ever seen. When the woman smiled her cheeks moved up, narrowing her eyes becomingly. Lora wanted to return her smile, so she did, and held out a hand. "You must be Payton. Cheyenne told us to expect you."

Payton grinned, looking back and forth between the two of them and Lora fought not to shift guiltily. It was obvious they'd just showered. Lora thought she would choke on her embarrassment, but she took a deep breath to ease it.

Payton took her hand and shook. "I am indeed. And you must be Lora. I've heard a lot about you, as well. Not sure why we never met in person before, though. Welcome to the round-up."

Turning, the woman scraped out one of the roasting pans into the garbage disposal. "I took fajita mix and tortillas out to the crew. Breakfast is covered tomorrow but they're only a few miles away now. They'll be here by lunchtime. I'll try to get up in time to be here when they get here, but I'm tired." She glanced at the clock on the wall. "I have just enough time to get home, shower and go into work."

"Are you okay to do that?" Lora asked.

Payton shrugged. "I've done it before. I'll catch up on sleep in the morning. Or maybe next week when the round-up is done," she laughed. Rinsing the pan, she set it on a dish-towel to dry, then moved to the second, but Lora waved her away.

"I can do this. Go do what you need to do."

Grinning, the shorter woman gave her a mock salute. "Yes, ma'am. It was nice meeting you, Lora. I always wondered what kind of woman it would take to rope a Lowell brother. Night guys."

"You better give that mouth a rest, girl," Chad growled.

Giggling, Payton headed for the front door. "Whatever, Lowell. Maybe I'll go harass your brother."

After she was gone, the kitchen turned quiet. Lora looked around. It was obvious Payton had cooked a lot of food to take out to the crew. The food wrappers were gone but there were still a few dishes. She began running soapy water into the heavy kitchen sink. "What does Payton do?"

"You mean other than be a pain in my ass?" Chad snorted. "We always thought she was going to run her father's breeding operation across the county, but she went on to school and is a paramedic for the local squad. She's been Cheyenne's best friend forever and they're thick as thieves. She's also Cheyenne's girls' godmother."

"Did you and she ever..."

Chad's eyes bulged. "Seriously? Hell, no. She's like my sister. Besides, I think Brock is kind of attached to her. Or wants to be. They've been dancing around each other for years."

Lora's brows rose. Brock was so forbidding and Payton seemed engaging. That could be an interesting relationship to watch.

Lora cleaned the kitchen and poured a glass of ice tea from the fridge, then followed Chad to the porch. Jackson seemed to have been waiting for them because he walked Mercy toward the house, long strides shortened so that he wouldn't leave her in the dust. Mercy peppered him with questions until she caught sight of her mother. "Mom, we trimmed hooves and braided tails and manes and stuff. That was interesting."

"Good job," she told her girl.

Mercy grinned, looking up at Jackson. Uh oh, looked like a bit of hero worship there.

"Jackson, can I get you a glass of tea?"

"No, thank you, Lora. I need to get home and clean up. I've got enough dirt on me for my own garden." He turned and started away. "Mercy, come see me tomorrow sometime."

"Okay!"

Lora loved seeing the relaxed look on her daughter's face. If she looked in a mirror, she had a feeling her own expression had eased, especially after their loving upstairs. She glanced at Chad. He had his head tipped back against the chair's headrest, eyes closed, and seemed to be on the verge of falling asleep. The glass of tea hung precariously in his hand. It was obvious he'd had a fulfilling day as well.

"I think we need to head to bed," she told Mercy. "And you need a shower before you even think about climbing between the sheets."

"Yes, ma'am."

Lora looked at her, wondering if a Texas twang could be picked up within just a few days. "Head on in. Tomorrow is going to be a huge day." She leaned down for a hug. "I love you, baby."

"I love you too, Mom."

Lora watched her daughter head into the house and kick off her new boots, marveling that she still had the energy to run up the stairs. Turning back to Chad, she reached out and took the glass of tea slipping from his hand, but he woke up, clutching at the glass. "Oh, sorry, babe."

Lora giggled. "I think we need to go to bed, cowboy."

Chad reached up to tip his non-existent hat. "Yes, ma'am."

Damn. Two ma'am's in less than thirty seconds. Tugging him up by the hand she led him into the house.

～

CHAD SLEPT LIKE THE DEAD, barely moving, and woke up stiff and aching. Jackson and Brock had tried to kill him. No, Jackson and Brock had gotten a job done that needed done. The cattle and all the people working them would be arriving soon, and there was a very good chance that his father would get to come home today as well. Just thinking about everything going on within the next few hours made him tired.

Rolling his head on the pillow, he looked for Lora. She was gone. And there was a hint of coffee and bacon in the air. He stretched, bones popping and muscles stretching. His hand landed on his hard dick. Maybe if he worked diligently today and came home and showered Lora would model for him again tonight. That was a long ways away, though, and he needed to get his ass moving. The sun was almost up already.

Chad retrieved the prosthetic sleeve from the bathroom and got dressed, then headed downstairs. Lora was in the kitchen sipping a cup of coffee. She smiled when she saw him and crossed the kitchen for a kiss. Chad was loving the new routine they were settling into.

"I put a plate in the microwave to keep warm for you."

"Is Mercy up yet?"

Lora shook her head, grinning. She wore another pair of those hip-hugging jeans today and he leaned back enough to look at her shirt. It was another short-sleeved button down, this one white with little pink and green flowers all over it. He raised an eyebrow at her, nodding approvingly, then pulled out the V of the shirt enough that he could look down at her bra. All he saw were the mounds of her flesh. "Do you even have a bra on?"

Giggling, she nodded, undoing a couple of the buttons. Glancing around to make sure they were alone, she pulled the sides apart long enough to give him a glimpse. Today she wore a tan bra, almost skin colored, but the cups were only half the size they normally were. The thing pushed her boobs up and out, till they almost popped out. He thought he saw the edge of a nipple. "Is that comfortable?"

She nodded. "Surprisingly, it is."

"I have to say babe, your tits look awesome."

Laughing outright, she leaned up for a kiss, rubbing those tempting mounds against his chest. Finally, he had to step back. "If I don't get my ass moving right now I won't be able to. You're too tempting. Can we postpone this till tonight? I promise to have enough energy for you."

With a seductive smile, she nodded. "You'd better."

Chad ate his breakfast, then gave her a last kiss. "I'm not sure what I'll be doing today, but the holding pens are just to the North if you need anything."

She nodded. "Okay. I found a bunch of chicken breasts in the freezer out in the garage. I'll marinate and grill them up and come up about noon. What else should I bring?"

Chad looked around the kitchen. "Mom had big cooler jugs somewhere she brings tea up in, or Lemonade. And maybe a cooler of just water."

"Done. I'll have Mercy help me. Any idea when your parents will be here?"

He shook his head. "I figure Cheyenne will send us a message when she leaves Amarillo. I'll forward you anything I receive."

He leaned down for another kiss. "I love you babe. Thank you for helping out like this."

"Of course. I wouldn't rather be anywhere else."

CHAPTER 13

LORA ALMOST ATE those words five hours later. She'd told Chad she would be there by noon, but it wasn't going to happen. Everything was behind. She thought she'd left enough time to grill all of the chicken breasts, and gather the condiments, buns, and make the drinks. Feeling generous she made a double batch of brownies, as well. And made fresh peach tea. She had no idea how many people she would be feeding today, but hopefully she had enough food and drink.

Malone Corporation work had fallen by the wayside. She'd responded to a couple of emails marked urgent, but that was it. None of her classwork had been completed.

She tried to tell herself that feeding the crew was the more immediate need, and her mind allowed her to shirk the other responsibilities. Mercy had helped where she could, but there was a lot Lora had to do herself.

While she was waiting for the brownies to finish baking she went through the house, looking for laundry that she might need to get started. She felt a little bad letting herself into Francine and Garrett's bedroom, but she didn't want Francine to have to deal with anything other than Garrett when they got home. Plus, Cheyenne had piqued her curiosity with her description the other day.

Their bedroom was a wonderland. Soft gray carpet cushioned her feet as she walked into the room. Romantic, gauzy fabric surrounded a large, four-poster bed with a lavender mattress skirt and a gray coverlet. The bed was perfectly made. As she looked around, Lora realized Garrett really had done his best to make the room feel like Paris. The walls were a soft gray but the far wall was pink and white striped. The white, distressed furniture was contemporary, but had been made to look aged. He had built her a small book nook with a built-in lounge, with a gray cushion and a small lamp table beside it. Old and new books lined the shelves and there were little tchotchkes here and there. Then, on the wall opposite the bed was a huge Eiffel Tower decal. It dominated the room, but didn't overwhelm it.

She peered into the bathroom and gasped. A modern freestanding tub took up one wall and there was a shower alcove for Garrett. Or maybe he liked baths too, Lora thought with a grin. It was definitely big enough for two. The room was painted a darker shade of gray than the bedroom, but matched perfectly. It still had that old romance feel from the bedroom. Beneath her feet were dark gray wood looking tiles.

Lora was impressed. She gathered up the few items of clothing she found in the hamper. As she closed the door and padded down the stairs she snorted. Who would have thought Garrett would have such a romantic streak for his wife?

The timer on the oven went off just as she finished loading the washer. When she returned from the camp she could transfer everything to the dryer.

Mercy came pounding down the stairs.

"Just in time," Lora grinned. "Let's get this stuff loaded. Can you help me?"

They piled everything in the back of Chad's truck. Just as they were getting ready to leave, Cheyenne pulled down the drive in her Jeep. Garrett sat in the front with her, scowling. Lora could see Francine and Emily in the back.

As the truck slowed to a stop, Lora stepped forward to open Garrett's door. "Hello," she said cheerfully. "You broke out of jail, huh?"

His right arm was braced on cushions and bandaged to his body. It looked supremely uncomfortable. Bracing his one good hand on the dashboard, he was able to swing his legs around, then step out. Francine edged around her to balance him.

Garrett looked out around the ranch. "Doesn't look like anything burned down while I was gone."

Lora laughed. "You know your sons wouldn't let that happen, Garrett."

He sighed and looked a little sad for a moment. "I know," he admitted.

Lora thought he probably wished there had been some visible sign that he'd been missed. If everything ran like clockwork when the manager was away, then how important was the manager?

"We were just taking lunch up to the holding pens, wherever they are."

His bright blue eyes brightened. "I could show you the way."

Lora turned to Francine, who jumped in immediately. "There's no way you're bouncing your happy ass up to that windmill, in any way, shape or form. You just got out of the hospital and have been ordered to sit and *rest*. It was bad enough we had to ride home with this fool daughter of ours."

"Hey," Cheyenne cried indignantly. "I took it slow just for you guys."

"And still managed to hit a curb and run a red light."

"It was ye-orange," she protested, laughing. "Believe me, Mama, it would have been worse if I'd have hit the brakes. Between you leaning between the seats the entire time fussing and Daddy fighting the seatbelt, one or both of you would have hit the dash."

"It was on the wrong side," he grumbled.

Francine sighed. "Yes, you're probably right, Cheyenne dear."

Cheyenne glanced over their heads and winked audaciously at Lora. It reminded her so much of Chad doing the same thing she burst out laughing.

Mercy stepped forward to hug her grampa and grandma. Lora was amazed at the love she could see from the older couple as they gushed over her daughter's new outfit.

Emily appeared from the back of the car, suitcase in hand. Lora thought she looked a little green around the gills, too. Maybe she was just imagining things but Emily definitely looked ill at ease as she looked around the yard.

Lora waited long enough to make sure they got into the house okay before making her goodbyes. "I'm already late," she admitted.

Garrett stretched an arm out toward the left side of the house. "Head in that direction toward the trees and you'll find the pens. If the cattle are there, you can't miss it."

Lora gave him a kiss on the cheek and herded Mercy out the door. Maybe she could take some pictures for him on her phone.

Lora hoped Chad didn't mind her driving his nice truck out on the range. There had only been one other truck outside and it had been as nice as Chad's, but she didn't know who it belonged to. So, Chad's truck went off-road.

They'd driven a couple miles down a barely there pitted dirt track when the haze came into the distance. Lora frowned, wondering if she was seeing right. Yes, it was definitely a dust cloud. Within a mile she crested a small rise and was able to look down upon the melee. Red coated cattle with white faces milled everywhere, not really heading in a direction but anxious. People on horseback surrounded the herd, some working to keep the cattle in line, others slouched lazily in the saddle just watching. It looked like they were slowly funneling them into a huge panel corral. Was that monstrous thing what Chad had been building yesterday?

There were a couple of smaller pens adjoining the big one, and there were people working inside it. Lora tried to see Chad, but it was just impossible. She couldn't even see the windmill or the supposed trees.

"Do you see him?" she asked Mercy.

Her daughter had released the seatbelt to lean into the windshield, looking down. "Nope. Don't see him yet."

There was a semi and a few other trucks parked off toward the right and the smaller corrals, so she headed slowly in that direction. She wasn't going to be responsible for spooking any of the cattle.

"There he is," Mercy cried, pointing.

Even pointing it took Lora a minute to recognize her fiancé galloping toward her up the slope on a bright coppery red horse with white feet. He had his hat tight to his head and the reins held loosely in one hand. Lora slowed the truck and just watched him.

Chad had always been a sexy man, but something about the way he looked now sent a shiver through her. He was in his element now and he looked so natural here. Yes, he was handsome walking down a street in Denver or shoveling snow from a sidewalk, but here there was an animation to his countenance that she'd never seen before.

She could see the bright white of his smile as he pulled to a stop beside the truck. He winced as he looked at the dusty exterior, then grinned, shrugging lightly. "Hey, Baby. Glad you made it out fine. If you follow me I'll show you where you can set up."

With an invisible touch to the reins he wheeled the horse around and trotted down the slope. He headed in the same direction she had, just a little more to the right. Lora cursed as she drove over some of the most rutted land she'd hit yet. It was a relief to get around to the other side and find the expanse of shade trees. A windmill blew a little crazily above them, squeaking rhythmically. Several trucks had been loosely circled so that the tailgates were inside the circle.

Chad pointed to show her where to park and she did, climbing out of the cab with a sigh. Chad was already off the horse and reaching for her.

Lora didn't care that he was dusty and dirty and had gross things on him. She loved him and wanted her greeting. So, reaching up, she tugged him close.

If he'd just dropped a peck on her lips, she would have been okay, but instead he pulled her close for a long, lingering kiss. Flinging her arms around his neck, she held him tight and kissed him right back, until someone cleared their throat. Chad let her go slowly, reluctantly, a grin on his face. Turning, he snatched Mercy into his arms and swung her around. "Hey, caterpillar. Did you have fun bouncing out here?"

She giggled, smacking him on the shoulders to let her down. "No! It was too bouncy. Why do you have to do it way out here?"

She looked around at the grassland.

"Well," Chad said slowly. "This is actually pretty close to

the highway. There's a little lane that the loaded semi can drive on to get to the main road."

Nodding, squinting in the bright sun, she looked around until he pointed where the lane was. The semi was already parked on it, ready to go when it was loaded.

Lora moved to the back of the truck and dropped the tailgate. The coolers were no worse for the wear. She pulled a sleeve of red Solo cups from a box, filled one with peach tea from one of the jugs and handed it to Chad.

Mouth going slack, he took it and drank it down. The second cup he drank a little more slowly. "That's great, babe. You just get parched out here. I know that will go fast."

Word apparently got out that the food had arrived, because people started wandering in. Then the riders came in. Mercy stood in the back of Chad's truck and handed out foil wrapped chicken sandwiches and bottles of water to those that needed to go back out. For a while Lora worried whether or not she would have enough, especially when most of the men took two sandwiches, but eventually the traffic slowed.

Everyone that paused long enough to introduce themselves to her was very nice, and she was surprised how many women were on the drive.

Chad shrugged when she mentioned it to him. "When Dad was a cowboy, women didn't really run cattle like this, but times have changed. It's still the men doing most of the heavy lifting and stuff, but the women are invaluable."

"I'll run cattle like this one day," Mercy said, flashing him a grin. Chad grinned right back at her. "I know you will, darlin'. Maybe we'll get you on a horse tomorrow and see what we can do."

Mercy's eyes widened and she almost fell out of the truck when she started bouncing around. Lora laughed at her daughter's joy, even as her heart cringed in fear. This was a dangerous job up here. She'd seen more than one cowboy limping, and one had had a bleeding gash on his thumb from catching it on a piece of metal. This wasn't a safe place for children.

Cheyenne kind of blew that theory out of the water half an hour later. She and her three daughters arrived wearing jeans, hats and boots, looking ready to work. Payton rode next to her, looking natural on the back of a huge black horse that seemed to float everywhere he walked. As soon as they arrived, they were ushered into the smaller round pen.

"Let's get to work, people," Brock called.

"Well," Chad said regretfully, "the break is over. Brock knows how to crack the whip on these cowboys. I'll show you where you can hang out and watch."

Leading them across the pasture he motioned to the tail-gate of a pickup backed right up to the fence. Nobody was there so Lora and Mercy climbed up in.

"I have to get back to work but you can watch everything from here for a while. These are the older calves getting shots. The bull calves get cut, meaning castrated. Snipped. And then they get branded as Blue Star cattle. This is bloody and messy. If it's too rough for Mercy you can take my truck back to the house and I'll see you tonight. Love you girls!"

Leaning up he gave her a kiss and a grin, then turned to get back on his horse. He rode to the far side of the small corral and he parked himself inside, blocking the cattle milling outside a panel gate. Every once in a while he would lean down and let a group of calves in, then shut the gate behind them. Two men on horseback inside the corral then roped the animals and dragged them over toward where Cheyenne had taken over a medical area. One of the wranglers would take the calf to the ground and tie up a rear leg so that a second man, Lora assumed a veterinarian, could cut the calf's scrotum to castrate him. Cheyenne moved in and gave the calf shots, then Carolyn, Cheyenne's oldest daughter, moved in with the branding iron to press it to the calf's flanks.

It was not a good day to be a young calf on the Blue Star.

One woman in particular caught Lora's eye, because she kept riding up to Chad while he was operating a gate letting calves in. The flashy palomino she rode had a mane the same color as the woman's curly blonde locks. She wore a bedazzled shirt that apparently repelled dirt, because there wasn't a speck on her. Making the horse dance, she moved around like she was trying to look busy. More than once, though, Lora saw Jackson and Brock send her dirty looks.

Tara Johnson hadn't changed. The first time Lora and Mercy had been to the ranch, she'd been up at the old foreman's cabin sniffing around Chad and he'd had to shut her down. Lora felt kind of bad because Derek's men had bound and gagged her, stealing her truck so that Chad wouldn't be alarmed when it came up the drive that rainy night.

She'd gotten loose, luckily, and found Brock, so it had all turned out well. Actually, if Brock hadn't arrived when he did, rifle in hand, things might have turned out very different for them all that wild night.

Though the woman was trying hard, Lora wasn't worried about Chad. He'd proven to her over and over again how much he loved her. If he was willing to literally put his life on the line for her and Mercy, how could she doubt him? In the intervening time since the attack he'd only gotten better, being steady and strong and patient, exactly as she needed him to be. He had a hell of a sense of humor, and they hadn't laughed in all their lives as much as they had with Chad in their lives.

But... what had *she* done to prove to him how much she loved *him*?

That thought sent a chill through her, because honestly,

she hadn't done much. In the time since he'd help her break free from Derek once and for all, she'd started pulling away. Not emotionally, she still loved him desperately, but he'd given her freedom in the ability to make decisions not based on fear anymore. He'd given her the ability to see the world and actually live her life. And the effect on Mercy had been even more profound. When they'd been dodging Derek, their emotions had been caustic. Fear, doubt, anxiety all in self-perpetuating loops. Now, everything was completely different and those loops broken open. Her daughter was learning to engage in life. Mercy connected with people more easily than Lora ever had. And she hadn't been fearful in a very long time.

Lora looked at her daughter. She had grown half a foot in the past few months, and put on healthy weight. She looked more like an eight year old should. Her green eyes were clear as they watched the commotion in the pen, and the shadow of fear was long gone.

"This isn't too gross for you, baby?"

Mercy didn't even spare her a glance, just leaned further over the top of the fence. "Nope," she said matter-of-factly, "I'm good. I need to learn what they're doing if I'm helping tomorrow."

For a moment, Lora stared at her daughter, amazed at the maturity in those words and most especially, Mercy's actions. The sight of the blood and the cries of the animals put Lora on edge. This situation was so far out of her element it wasn't even funny. Mercy, on the other hand, seemed to be acclimating like ranching was in her blood. Mercy was, quite literally, ready to jump into the Lowell family.

Lora admired her daughter's courage.

Oh, hell.

Her mind returned to her previous question. What *had*

she done to show Chad how much she loved him? She told him everyday. But there was a devil's advocate in her conscience bitching at her, doubting that assertion, because did she actually tell him that every day over the past year and change since she'd fallen in love with him? When she was hip deep in alligators trying to save the company and pass her classes? No, she hadn't. She knew she hadn't, and it was killing her to admit it.

From this point on she was going to be the best woman she could be to Chad. She looked down at the ring on her finger. The white gold solitaire shone as brightly as the night he'd given it to her. But it needed a companion ring. It needed a wedding band. She *wanted* a wedding band.

She glanced across at the woman on the prancing palomino. If Chad had a matching band on his finger it would probably cut down on a lot of these incidents. It was time she collected on the promise he'd made them, to love and protect her forever. And to always have starlight mints at the ready. She'd have to ask him for one next time they were together.

LORA HEADED BACK to the ranch, an idea percolating in her head, and she wondered if they could pull it off.

Unpacking the truck took a while and Francine came out to help. Garrett sat in the family room in a well-worn leather recliner, punching buttons on a remote. When Lora got a moment, she went in to talk to him and share the pictures she'd taken with her phone.

"The corral looks good," he said gruffly.

"Chad and Jackson and Brock did that yesterday."

She'd taken several pictures of the older calves and some

of the new babies, interspersed with pictures of the hands helping out.

"Francine, come look at these," Garrett called.

Chad's mother smiled as she leaned over him, her hand resting protectively on his good shoulder. "Oh, look at those pretty babies."

"I wish I could be out there helpin'," he murmured.

There was one picture of Cheyenne with her long leg thrown over a red calf, tying his feet together. Carolyn, her oldest daughter, was handing her something. Their faces were gritty and determined, and exceptionally beautiful, red hair flying around their faces. Garrett looked at that one for a long time. "Those are my girls, Lora," he said proudly, and there was the glimmer of tears in his eyes.

She showed him the one of Mercy with her arm thrown around Grace, their hats leaning together, bright hair beneath spilling down their shoulders. "More of my girls," he said firmly. "Mercy fits in like she's always been here."

"She does," Lora agreed. "Chad isn't technically her father but they have so many of the same likes and dislikes."

"He's her father in every way important," Francine told her firmly.

Lora nodded. "Yes, he is." She took a deep breath. "I need to think about a few things, but I might have a favor to ask of you guys soon."

Francine smiled and rested a hand on her own. "Whatever you need, dear. You've helped us so much this week I can't even begin to thank you."

Lora frowned. "I don't need to be thanked. We're in Denver, but we're still family. I consider you family, anyway."

"Oh, we do too, Lora, of course we do. We just don't want to impose on your life anymore than we already have."

"I'm sorry about all this mess," Garrett told her, his eyes regretful.

"Would you two stop? Please? I love you guys, and I know Mercy does too. We wouldn't rather be anywhere else right now. Now, I'm going to go come up with something clever for dinner for all of us. Francine, do you mind if we use your hot tub later tonight?"

Her pale eyes lit up. "Absolutely not. Use it all you want!"

CHAPTER 14

CHAD SIGHED as Tara jostled her horse into his own. It was unnecessary and dangerous, and he was getting tired of being nice.

"Tara, I need you to replace Ian on the back side," Jackson told her as he reined up beside them. "His horse threw a shoe and he's getting it fixed."

Chad was never so glad to see the foreman and his big-assed paint. Once again he was where he needed to be when, and it worked in Chad's favor. If he'd had to deal with Tara a minute longer he would have snapped and said things that would *not* be cool. Tara used to be a friend and he didn't want to ruin relations between their neighboring families. There were as many Johnson ranch hands here today as Lowell.

"No, you can send someone else."

She wheeled her horse around, expecting that to be the end of it, but the big paint moved in front of her. "No," Jackson said smoothly. "There's a hole in the line that needs filled. You are my spare outrider. All you're doing here is spooking the calves. Move down the line or go home, because you're no use to me right now."

With a fling of her hair, she turned the horse toward the outside of the corral and galloped away, spooking more cattle as she passed.

Jackson sighed. "That girl is a pain in my ass."

"You? You ought to be in my seat right now," Chad laughed. "Oh, Chad," he mocked in a sing-song voice like Tara's, "when you wear gloves you can't even tell you're not normal any more."

Jackson laughed. "That's not bad. She once told me I'd better be grateful that the Lowell family had taken me in because otherwise I would be an alcoholic on a reservation somewhere."

Chad winced, shaking his head. "Well, at least she doesn't discriminate handing out her discrimination. I thought I was the only one lucky enough to get her little jabs."

"No," Jackson sighed. "We all get it. And she seems oblivious. Still."

"Well, thank you. I was reaching my breaking point."

"I know." With a tip of his black hat, Jackson turned and rode away.

Chad glanced up, looking for Lora through the dust. Had she seen Tara's little performance?

She was gone. Mercy was still there in the back of the truck and Grace, Cheyenne's littlest, was sitting with her, but Lora had disappeared. He glanced out to the right. His truck was gone as well. Damn it! Dealing with Tara and her shenanigans had cost him seeing where his fiancée had gone, or even when. Had she seen Tara flirting and taken off because he'd been just trying to ignore it?

The thought worried him all day. In order to get the steers done, they needed to work into the evening. It was almost eight by the time they got back to the ranch, bedraggled and tired. Chad looked for Lora, though, hoping that she would come out to meet them.

There she was. Sitting on the front porch with his mom and dad. He urged the horse up to the porch and reached behind him for Mercy's arm. She'd ridden behind him all the way home, chattering a mile a minute.

He lowered her to the ground and she ran up the steps to share her day. Lora looked up at him and smiled. He wiggled a finger at her and she stepped down onto the bottom step, close enough that he could lean down and kiss her.

"I missed you, babe," he growled.

She grinned at him. "You were busy dodging bottle blondes."

He sighed, shaking his head. "That woman, she's never going to learn. It was bad today and I'm sorry you had to see that. It means nothing to me, I hope you realize that."

Lora nodded. "I know. I think it's sad actually."

"I hope she finds someone, I really do."

"Maybe she'll find a hobby. Go put your horse away," she told him, patting the red rump. "Then get your shower. I'll have a plate ready for you when you come down."

"Oh woman, I do love you so!"

"Love you too, Chad."

Before he could put the horse away, though, he had to answer Dad's questions about what was going on up at the camp. Yes, they had enough inoculant for the amount of cattle left to be done. Yes, they had had enough hands today. No, no injuries. Yes, he'd watched all the girls when they were in with the calves to make sure they were being safe. No, the semi hadn't gotten stuck like it had last year.

Chad wished there was a way his father could take part in the round-up, but there just wasn't. The ground was too rough for him to even drive up in a truck, let alone walk on with all of the cattle ruts. If he fell, he would break his arm all over again and that just couldn't happen.

Chad took his time answering his father's questions because if he had been in the same position he would be doing the same thing. Finally, his father seemed out of questions. "Dad, I need to get Oakley cooled off."

His father waved at him with his left hand, but Chad could see the disappointment in his eyes. It was going to be a long recovery for Garrett Lowell.

Oakley appreciated the attention. Chad tied him to the outside post and picked the dirt from his hooves then hosed him down, sluicing all the sweat away with the blade of his hand. Oakley loved the water and bobbed his head when Chad hosed down his neck. He talked to him the entire time and Oakley seemed to enjoy the noise.

Just as he was finishing up, Brock pulled in with the flatbed truck. Rather than walk straight past Chad on the way in to the barn as he normally did when Chad was home, he paused. "You've done good work the past couple of days. Wasn't sure if you'd remember what to do."

"Of course I remembered," Chad laughed. "I did this stuff my entire childhood."

"Yeah, I know, but it's been a few years since you had to go at it so hard."

"True. I didn't do nearly what you and Jackson did, though. Only about half the work," he joked, waving his weak hand.

Brock huffed, shaking his head as he looked at the ground. "Not sure why you joke about it but I thought you kicked ass. I'd hire you as a hand any time."

Chad wanted to laugh, but he really and truly appreciated that sentiment. His big brother's good opinion meant a lot to him, it always had. "Thank you for that, Brock. I appreciate it."

"Luckily," his brother continued, crossing his heavy arms, "you're family and I don't have to pay you shit."

Chad stared for a moment, then burst out laughing. "You know, I was just going to return the compliment and tell you what a fantastic horse this was, but now I'll keep it to myself."

Brock grinned, looking like the light-hearted brother he used to be. "He is pretty nice, isn't he? I trained him for you, you know."

Turning, Brock headed into the barn. Chad stared at his brother's back. Wait, what? He had trained the horse for Chad?

Tugging Oakley's lead line, he followed Brock into the barn. The colt went into his stocked stall happily, snatching hay before Chad was even out the door. Then he went to look for his confusing brother.

"What do you mean you trained the horse for me?"

Brock looked up from the mare he was cooing to as he brushed her heavy belly. Twisting his mouth, he sighed, looking down at her. "I realized the first time you were here with Lora... hell, even before that. When you first started riding again after you'd been injured you had issues getting on a horse the regular way. They're trained to accept a rider from one side only, and when you break that habit it puts them off. I watched you fight with horses every time you rode, because they usually spooked when you got on them from the other side. I assume your leg can't twist the way it used to or something, right?"

Chad nodded, stunned at what was coming out of his brother's mouth.

"So, I trained a couple horses to be, I dunno, ambidextrous. I knew you'd like Oakley, though." He looked up with a grin. "You always liked the bright sorrels like that."

"I did," Chad agreed. He stared at Brock, wondering when the aliens had abducted him. Had to have been within the past two years. This wasn't the same Brock he was used to. "You did a great job with him."

Brock shrugged. "There's an equine therapy program for veterans that opened up a few miles away. I've trained a few mustangs for them and donated them."

Brock wouldn't meet his eyes, and for the first time, Chad was glad of that. It gave him a chance to gather his emotions. He coughed to clear his throat. "You're working with veterans?"

That shrug again. It seemed strange to see his older brother at a loss for words. "Just here and there. Went over to ask to see what would make it easier for you and I realized they needed more animals."

"How many have you given them?"

Brock scratched under the mare's belly and she lowered her head with a sigh. Chad reached out and stroked her forelock from her eyes, rubbing the white star on her head.

"About ten, eleven. Something like that. The BLM is loving me right now because I'm actually doing something with the animals they foster with me."

Chad was absolutely floored. Was this why his brother had softened to him recently? Because he'd been working with other veterans?

"And a few times a month, when they get short-handed, I volunteer. Just helping out with basic riding instruction and stuff. No big deal."

Uh, it was a huge deal actually. Chad stared at the top of his brother's dusty black hat, trying to find words. But if he did find words, his damn throat was so tight he didn't know if he'd be able to say anything.

When military personnel returned from overseas, it was sometimes a huge integration process. In the past few years organizations had popped up to help them re-engage in society. Equine therapies seemed to be one of the most effective, though they were sometimes harder to get into. Very often those therapies survived only on private contributions, so the fact that Brock was supporting one was significant.

Chad had seen first-hand the impact equine therapy and canine therapy had on returned warriors.

"That's really something, Brock. I appreciate you doing that. The charities that help veterans need all the support they can get."

Brock glanced up, catching his eye. "Yeah, I know. And the guys seem to really appreciate getting out and riding. You can literally see the confidence building in them when they get on the back of a horse. It's made me appreciate even more what I do every day." He paused and glanced at Chad, giving him solid eye contact for a long moment. "I'm sorry I didn't understand what you needed when you came back. I guess I felt like I didn't know how to talk to you anymore. Working with these guys has really opened my eyes to some things. It started with the horses and now we just ... get along."

Chad blinked, his breath gone. He felt like the sweet-tempered, heavily pregnant mare had just mule-kicked him in the chest. But no, she still stood in the same place accepting the attention the brothers were giving her. Glancing down the aisle way, he looked for the ice. Nope, Texas hadn't frozen over. Brock apologizing to him for being a shit had never even occurred to him as being a possibility today.

"That's okay. I appreciate that you're getting me now, even if it is nine years later," he laughed.

Brock gave him a grin. "Hey, I'm trying little brother. Give me that, at least."

Chad let his smile fall away. "I am, Brock," he said seriously. "Thank you."

If he'd been closer he probably would have leaned in for a

manly hug, but maybe that was pushing it tonight. "Well, I'm going to go grab some dinner and talk to my woman. Will you be okay out here?"

Brock nodded. "I'll see you bright and early in the morning, little bro. No sleeping in."

"I don't know," Chad told him. "I'm not getting paid, so..."

He backed out of the stall to avoid the brush flying his way, but he laughed, easier than he had for a long time.

Chad hurried through his shower and getting dressed again. Rather than put the same sweaty boot prosthetic on and a pair of jeans, he pulled on a pair of jogging shorts and his blade prosthetic. Then he brushed his teeth and hair and hurried downstairs.

His mother did a double take at the sight of his blade, but she smiled. "You never used to want to wear the blade around here."

Chad shrugged, leaning down to press a kiss to her cheek. "Times change."

"Yes, they do," she sighed.

"You okay, Mama?"

She nodded. "Yes, just planning what to feed the crew tomorrow. Your father is asleep in the recliner. He won't be able to sleep in a bed for a long time, I don't think."

Chad frowned. "Really? Ah, because he can get up out of it easier," he mused. "Want us to move a recliner back to your bedroom? We've got a bunch to pick from. That way you can still sleep with him, kind of."

Her pale blue eyes turned luminous with tears and she nodded. "I think that would be a fabulous idea. Thank you for thinking of it."

"We'll do that tomorrow. You already have a TV back there and everything. He can be comfortable without other people around him."

She nodded and squeezed his arm. "I'm glad you're here, Chadwick. I've missed seeing you."

"I've missed seeing you too, Mama."

Turning to the microwave she removed a meal and handed it to him. "Lora is on the back patio. Go join her."

Chad did as he was told.

Lora looked up from her computer and smiled at him. "Hey, babe. Let me finish this email and I'll shut it down."

"You have a few minutes. It'll take me a while to get through all this food."

Lora grinned. "You can do it. I have faith in you."

Chad ate most of the food while Lora clattered on the keys of her Mac. The sun was just slipping down below the horizon, casting an orange glow over everything. He was almost done eating when his mother carried out two little plates of pie with whipped cream on top. "Thought you might want something sweet to end with."

Lora groaned. "I can tell I'm going to gain weight here," she laughed.

Francine grinned and winked at her, then returned to the house.

Chad cleaned his plate, then pulled the little plate in front of him. It wasn't whipped cream on top, it was meringue. Somewhere mom had picked up a lemon meringue pie. He groaned as he swallowed it down. "That's good."

Lora ate hers as well after she closed up her computer, and she looked at him with a smile in her eyes. "You look content. More than I've seen you in a long time."

Chad told her about the conversation with Brock and her eyebrows shot into her hairline. "Wow, that's really something. Sounds like he has a new understanding of your life now and what you've been through since you were injured."

Chad frowned. "I don't know. Maybe. We'll see what happens."

"Try to keep it lighthearted. I know he seems pretty dark, but it has to be a lot of responsibility taking on the running of the ranch, too. And if he was there when your dad went down, it had to be hard."

Yeah, it did. He'd probably thought Dad was dead when he saw him crumple like that. They'd had injuries on the farm before, some even worse than what had happened to Dad, but during the incident it had to be alarming.

He wished he'd been there for his brother, because he really didn't have anyone. If he'd open his eyes and look at Payton maybe that would change, but...

"Your brother is a strong man. If he has even a smudge of your strength of heart, he'll be fine."

Chad smiled at her crookedly. "I love you, baby. I really do. Thank you for everything you've done since you've been here too."

She shook her head. "I haven't done anything, really. But I'm about to."

With a slight grin she stood from the table and held her hand out to him. "Can I have a mint?"

Chad wondered at the intensity in her eyes. Something was going on, but he wasn't sure exactly what. He handed her one of the mints he had in his shorts pocket. She took it from his hand and looked at it for a long moment. "You told me you would always have a mint for me. No matter what. And that you would love me always."

When her eyes filled with tears he grew alarmed. Pushing to his feet he reached out to cup her cheek. "Of course, babe. What's going on?"

She looked at the ground, shaking her head. A crystalline tear dripped from her cheek to the ground, then another. "You've been a better partner than I have, and I'm sorry for that."

His stomach bottomed out. "You have nothing to apologize for. You're following your dream and securing a future for your daughter with Malone."

She shook her head again before looking up. "But that's wrong. I thought I was doing what was right but as I look back and realize how wonky things have gotten, I've realized *you* are the most important part of the equation. *You* are what's secured her future, not the money I'm making or the legacy I'm building. You have had more of an impact, positive of course, on her life than anything I've done."

"You're her mother," he disagreed. "She looks up to you for everything."

Lora smiled sadly. "She used to, but she's grown so much since we met you. She's learned that it's okay to rely on another person, and I'm so thankful that you are that person, Chad. In this one thing I am more of a child than my own daughter. I know this sounds a little defeatist, but I'm not meaning it to be. The good part is coming, I promise."

She flashed him a smile and his tension eased incrementally, but he could still see the turmoil that had turned her eyes dark green. It made his heart ache for her. She'd been struggling with something for a while. "You know I love you dearly. Speak your heart."

Her smile lit up her face. "When I got together with you it was a very disconcerting experience. I had never relied so heavily on any man before. I think I expected you to bail at any minute. I immersed myself in the corporation and the class work, but I've come to realize that it was all a shield." She reached up to stroke his cheek. "I was actually avoiding the relationship with you. I didn't want to believe that you were as perfect as you seemed, and that you could actually love broken down, soiled me."

Chad started to protest but she held up a slender hand. "I know you don't see me like that, but in my mind I do, I *did*. I was in an abusive marriage longer than the two of us have been together, so it's taken me a while to even contemplate being a whole, independent woman. And I think I've unconsciously delayed making the final commitment to you, marriage, for a couple of reasons. The first being I've enjoyed being in charge of this huge corporation. It's a bit of poetic justice. I'm running the company that once financed the attempted abduction of my daughter."

Chad wasn't sure he liked the look in her eyes. It was a little frantic and glossy, like she was remembering the trauma, but she focused her gaze back on his and the vagueness disappeared.

"And I think the second reason was because I always expected you to find someone better than me." Her eyes filled with tears but she tipped her head back to keep them from falling. "But you're not looking for better than me. When I watched that Tara woman flirting with you for hours, and your non-response, it suddenly hit me that I've never had worries about you physically cheating on me. It's always been my fear of not being enough for you."

She ran her hands through her long hair, looking out over the land. "I came out here, though, and things have become clear. Cheyenne mentioned a few things to get me thinking, and I've noticed others. I've had my head in the sand for a long time and I apologize to you for that."

Chad stroked her cheek, almost overcome with emotion. "I didn't want to push you because I didn't want to set off the same triggers your ex did. Even when you were lost in your work I still loved you dearly. But I definitely hoped," he grinned, "that you would cut back a little and remember we were still here waiting for you."

Tears rolled down her cheeks, but he swiped them away with his thumbs, pressing a kiss to her forehead.

"I've woken up," she promised him. "I'm seeing everything I'm supposed to be seeing. And I love you more than I ever have." She looked up at him, her eyes clearing. "Which brings me to the point of this conversation."

Lora grinned at him and stepped back, holding his hand high for a moment, as if in a dance move. Then she dropped to one knee in front of him, posing. She held out the starlight mint like a ring. "Chadwick Lowell, you have the patience of a saint and I wish you'd kicked me in the ass sooner to wake me up to what I was doing to our family. I love you more than I ever expected to and I love you more today than I did yesterday. Thank you for being the man and father that you are. I hope you will agree to marry me again. But this time, with a definite wedding date."

She was still smiling by the time she came to the end, but he could see the anxiety in her eyes. He lifted her to her feet as quickly as he could. "You know I love you dearly and I would wait years for you to be ready for marriage. I wasn't pushing you because you're worth waiting for. I will say, though, I'm glad you've recognized a few things. I don't think I'm cut out to talk to Mercy about boys, or boobs. Or periods. Oh, hell, to the no."

They laughed together and it was as natural as breathing to reach for each other. They just hugged for several long moments, before Lora drew back. "I'm glad you said yes, because I've kind of been pondering an idea. What do you think about having your dad plan the wedding?"

Chad reared back as if he'd been kicked by a longhorn. This was apparently the night to test his constitution. "Wh-what? *Dad?*"

Lora nodded, her jaw firming. "Your father is going stir crazy not being able to help out. You just saw a small part of what we dealt with today. The anxiety is very real for him, and probably not good for his recovering heart. What if we give him another job to do, to concentrate on something not physical so that he's not missing the ranch work? I'll pick my dress, but he can design the wedding." She looked up and out over his mother's lovingly-landscaped back yard. "I would be happy to have it here, sometime in the next few months. Fall, I think."

He took a deep breath, realizing how serious she was. This was a monumental step. He'd brought up getting married before, but she'd always had some *something* to get in the way. His heart swelled with pride.

"I can't commit a lot of time to planning it," she told him simply. "I've told William to take control this week, but soon my nose will be back to the grindstone. With a new purpose, though. I'm going to see about taking a back seat, if William is comfortable running it more long-term. He signed on under the expectation that I would eventually take over, but I don't want to do that any more. I love the business, I love seeing that I'm having a positive impact on it, but Garrett being injured has been a blessing in disguise. I just want to be with you guys. I've loved the past few days, hanging with Mercy and seeing a completely new side of you." Her eyes glinted with orneriness. "A new, sexy side of you."

Chad nodded. "Yeah, it's the horse sweat," he told her, deadpan. "It has natural aphrodisiac properties."

He laughed when she wrinkled her nose. "Honestly, it doesn't bother me too much. It has a very *you* flavor to it."

Leaning down, he kissed her on the lips, lingering when her mouth softened beneath his. Lora was right. The past few days had been a true reconnection and he wanted it to last. "Let's try to be very cognizant of our obligations and our priorities when we get home. Are you still going to get your business degree? I definitely think you should. You've put too much time and effort into it not to follow through."

"Yes, but I don't have to jam as many classes into my schedule as I have been. I felt like I was under a deadline, but I'm kind of letting that go. William is doing a great job with the company and he's hired great people to work under him. The immediacy to get in there and control every little item is still there, but being with you and Mercy is more important to me. The corporation could go under tomorrow and we would be fine, money wise. That's what I need to remember. When I was with Derek I had an emergency go-bag hidden in my bathroom, and I would save the spending money he would give me and I would squirrel it away for when I broke away. The practice worked for me that time, and it's hard not to squirrel more and more away."

He nodded, understanding. "I understand." Reaching out, he stroked her hair behind her ear. "Without sounding condescending I want to tell you I'm proud of you."

"Well, I've had some not so proud moments recently. Coming home and finding Denver PD babysitting your kid is not fun, even if he is a friend."

"Be glad it was Dean and not Rachel. She would have read you the riot act. Twice. Second time like a Marine."

"I know," she sighed. "And she would have been completely right to do so. You could have read me the riot act and I would have taken it."

"I know, but I could see the anxiety in your eyes. You didn't need me to verbalize it."

"No," she sighed. "You always know what to say or do, but I want you to know you can talk to me more. You don't always have to stuff everything down. You and your dad have that in common. You both steam," she laughed.

Chad frowned at her. "Whatever. I don't steam."

"Okay, stubborn."

They laughed together and it was free and easy, one of the most relaxed moments he could ever remember being in his life. Lora was the love of his life and they had a long future together. And it had taken them time, but they were more clear-eyed about finding the balance. "I love you, Lora. With every breath in my body."

"I love you, too, babe."

With a final kiss she turned and tugged him toward the house. "Let's go talk to your dad."

"Wait, you were *serious* about that?"

CHAPTER 15

"Emily."

Emily squeezed her eyes tight, cursing inwardly. She should have known that Jackson would be looking for her.

Naively, she'd thought he would be busy with the animals, or heading to his own house for dinner, because the truck he drove was gone. So she'd gone for a walk toward the paddocks, leaving her parents chatting on the porch. There was a temporary metal pipe corral set up against one of the paddocks, with a young horse inside it. It had been a long time since she'd been near horses, and she wanted to take advantage of the quiet time while she could. She had a couple of carrots in her pockets, to be broken up into pieces if the little horse would come to her.

She'd scanned the area diligently. No Jackson. She'd planned to visit the one horse, then return to the house.

But of course it couldn't be that easy.

Sucking in a huge breath of air, she turned around.

Holy crap. Even in the almost completely dark evening, she could see his huge form in the shine of the moon, and it sent a thrill through her. Jackson Windwalker was a large man, but he managed to walk like a ninja. It was why she hadn't heard him. It was why she *never* heard him, she thought with a quiet laugh. His name suited him so perfectly.

"Hello, Jackson. How are you?"

He reached out a hand to run a finger down her cheek, and her breath stalled in her chest. A rough thumb pad brushed over her lips. "I'm better now that I can see you."

Emily blinked, her heart taking off into a gallop. With just a few words he reminded her of so many things— love, laughter, racing the wind.

Reaching up, she cupped his broad hand in her own, then gently pulled it away. "I'm sorry, Jackson. I shouldn't have come out here and given you the wrong idea."

Years ago they'd met at the corrals for their midnight rides. It had been a secret thing they'd done every full moon.

She glanced up at the sky. Yep, a full moon. Had she subconsciously been aware of that?

There was a snuffling at her shoulder and she thanked the gods above for sending her a distraction. Trying not to move too fast, she turned to face the corral. A yearling filly stood a few inches away, ears pricked as she investigated the humans. Reaching into her pocket, Emily brought out one of the carrots and snapped off an end, then held the piece out to the little horse. Soft velvet lips brushed over her hand as the treat was taken, but the little horse tossed her head, unfamiliar with it, before she bit into it and began to chew. Emily chuckled as the horse moved her lips around, trying to get all the little pieces of carrot down.

The entire time, though, she could feel Jackson standing behind her. His heat and energy radiated out against her. When a finger brushed at the shell of her ear, pushing her loose hair away, she didn't move.

This was a terrible position to be in. Jackson had a heart the size of Texas, and she didn't want to hurt him for anything, but they couldn't just take up where they'd left off. She had obligations in Houston that she couldn't get out of.

It took a monumental effort to move a few millimeters away from the touch on her ear. "Please don't," she whispered. "I'm only here for a few days to help out, then I'm returning to Houston."

Rather than move away she felt him move closer to her back, blocking the slight breeze. Without touching her he lifted his arms and clasped the top pipe of the corral in his fists, effectively caging her in. His lips brushed at her ear. "A lot can happen in a few days," he whispered.

Emily clenched her eyes shut, her body taking up a tremor. She gripped the bar in front of her. "We can't, Jackson. Please don't do this. I can't do this."

The tip of his nose ran around the outside of her ear, and he leaned into her. "Why not?"

She hadn't wanted to let him know like this, but he left her no recourse. Just a few more seconds and she would be in serious trouble. "Because I'm engaged, Jackson."

For a moment nothing happened, then his arms fell away. He stood behind her silently for several long seconds before the cool air moved in against her back. When she opened her eyes, the engagement ring on her left hand blinked in the moonlight where she gripped the pipe. Turning around she looked for Jackson, but he was gone.

CHAPTER 16

L<small>ORA CLUTCHED</small> C<small>HAD'S HAND</small>, feeling jubilant. Francine and Garrett were still on the front porch, enjoying the moonlit evening. Porch lights glowed softly a few feet away. They looked up and both of them returned her wide smile. Garrett was finally beginning to lose his hospital pallor.

"Did you have a good dinner?" Francine asked.

Lora nodded her head, plopping down into the rocker that Chad pulled up for her. "We did, and we wanted to talk to you about some things. Garrett, have you ever planned a wedding?"

Garrett looked shocked. "A wedding? No, I've never planned a wedding."

"Would you like to?"

The older man blinked, scowled, then looked to Francine. She gave him a smile and a shrug.

"Let me tell you what we're thinking," Lora told him. "After the round-up is done, we're returning to Denver, but we've been talking. We want to get married, probably some-time in the fall. Not a big blowout or anything like that. Just a small intimate gathering, maybe even in your back garden if you don't mind."

"In my garden?" Francine gasped.

Lora nodded. "I love your garden and I know you've put a lot of time into it. It would be a beautiful setting for a ceremony, don't you think?"

Francine blinked. "It could be stunning. Oh, Garrett, we have so much work to do."

Chad held up a hand. "Now, we don't want you stressing about this. That wasn't why we approached you about it. We want this to be more party-like." He looked to Lora for confirmation and she nodded, encouraging him. "No big to-do. I would like to invite the Lost and Found guys and their families, some neighbors. Have a grill out, maybe. Oh, and a dance floor."

Lora felt bad because his parents seemed a little dazed. Maybe this was too much to approach them with. She'd wanted to give Garrett a purpose, but didn't want to overwhelm him. But then he smiled. No, he *grinned*, and life came into his eyes. "You would let us do this?"

"Yes. I get to pick out the dress but you can build the wedding around it. Would that be okay?"

Garrett nodded. "That sounds wonderful. Are you sure you trust us to do this?"

"I am. Because the little details don't matter to me, just that I'm married to Chad at the end of the ceremony."

Garrett glanced between them. "Well, then, you'll get your wedding."

"I'll call the accountant this week to set up a new account that you guys can pull from for expenses. I'll make sure I won't be able to see anything on it so that it will stay secret."

"Are you sure you want us to do this, Lora? A wedding is an important part of a woman's life."

She smiled at Francine, a little sad. "I had a wedding once

with all the trimmings, and it didn't pan out. I want it much more simple this time. More family oriented. I would love for Mercy to be involved somehow."

Francine retrieved a notepad from the house and they began making notes. Lora found that she had several strong ideas and *must haves*, more than she expected actually. And Chad had a few requests as well. Luckily, they were in line with each other.

By the time they began to wind down, the focus of Garrett's time looking forward was on the wedding. With his arm bandaged the way it was, though, it basically meant he was doing research.

"Have you ever used Pinterest?" Lora asked him.

"No. What's that?"

It took her another half hour to show him the Pinterest app on the brand-new-in-the-package-tablet Cheyenne had gotten him last year for his birthday, and that he'd never opened. It took Chad just a few minutes to set it up with an account and a new email, then start installing apps. Garrett found that by propping the tablet on his crossed knee he was able to operate it. And a whole new world opened up to him.

Mercy came out at one point and wished everyone a good night, then tromped up the stairs to her bedroom.

Chad and Lora eventually made their escapes, long after night had fallen. Garrett waved goodbye absently, but Francine blew them a kiss and mouthed 'thank-you'. Maybe if Garrett was absorbed in this, he wouldn't be so concerned with the ranch.

They headed into the house but Lora didn't let Chad go up the stairs. Instead she tugged him out the back door. She led him along the paver path to the hot tub gazebo on the back grass.

"Oh, what do you have in mind, future Mrs. Lowell?"

With a flirty glance she entered the gazebo, dropping her

shirt and jeans as she entered. Chad was right on her heels and he whistled when she turned to pose for him.

The one-piece pale green bathing suit should have been demure, and it was anything but. Her body was covered by a series of straps strategically placed to cover the naughty bits. It was a bit of a pain to get into. Before she climbed into the hot tub, she gave him a flirty look. "Your turn."

Chad scrambled out of his clothes. "No bathing suit, so I guess I have to go naked."

He dropped his drawers and she giggled. His dick was very happy to be there right at that moment. Chad took long enough to remove his prosthetic before slipping into the water with her.

She floated into his waiting arms.

"I think what you did tonight was incredible," he told her softly, pressing a kiss to her chin.

Lora's legs wrapped around his waist and his erection settled between her thighs. "I love you. I've loved you for a long time. Some things needed to happen to remind me of that fact, though, and I'm sorry about that."

"You know," Chad said thoughtfully. "Maybe we should have Forget-me-Nots at the wedding. Just in case."

She smacked him on the shoulder, laughing. "I poured my heart out tonight and you're making jokes."

"I just don't want you to take yourself too seriously," he laughed. "You've grown into a strong woman but now you need to loosen up. You're on a good path with these clothes and spur of the moment decisions. Now we need to work on sex in public."

He ground himself against her and she gasped. "We're not in public," she protested.

"No, but we're outside at least."

Pulling her toward him, he took her mouth in an erotic kiss. Lora sighed and her body responded as he spread his hands over her ass. One hand slipped between their bodies to pull the gusset of her bathing suit to the side. Then he began to guide his body into hers. "I love you, Lora."

"And I love you, Chad."

They made love slowly, rocking tight. At one point he floated them over to a straighter, shallower, reclining bench. It enabled Lora to sit up straighter on him, taking him deeper and deeper as she rode him. And when they found their release it was timed perfectly, both of them crying out at the same time. It was flawless.

There were a lot of things about to happen in their future, and Lora wasn't sure if she was ready for everything, but Chad would be there to guide her through it. They were starting with a solid base of love.

To be continued…

THE LOST AND FOUND SERIES

If this is your first time reading my work, you may want to check out the **Lost and Found Series**, where you can read Chad and Lora's original story Embattled Home. Every story is about combat-modified warriors finding love. The first two books are free, and you can find all of them here, at my website.

www.JMMadden.com

AFTERWORD

And for my regular readers-
You may have noticed a mention of Brian Calvert working
on Henry Bright's embezzlement case. Author Siobhan Muir
contacted me one day wondering if she could mention the
Lost and Found Group in her new release *Star Light, Star
Bright*. I told her sure, and that I would return the favor.
You'll have to stay tuned because yes, Brian Calvert will be
getting his own story!
In the mean time, if you'd like to check out Siobhan's work,
follow the links below!

And here's a blurb for *Star Light, Star Bright*

Sometimes the brightest stars need to come home… Henry
Bright has a picture-perfect life as a rising star in the country
rock scene—fortune, fame, and more lovers than he can
shake a stick at. But something is missing. The glitz of
Nashville is nothing more than glitter and tinfoil. Searching
for authenticity in his life, he completes his DVM in
veterinary medicine and returns to Wyoming. He takes a job

as a vet at the Triple Star Ranch, hoping to find meaning and connection. He just didn't expect to find love.

Trip Colton's wife died over thirty years ago and he figured that was it for love. But the moment he meets Henry, he can't get the younger man off his mind. The problem is, he's never been attracted to a man before and the realization throws him for a loop. Dating is hard at any age, but Trip's out of practice and wooing a man is completely different than wooing a woman.

When Henry's former manager, Jordie, tracks him to Wyoming and begs the star to come back to the music biz, tensions damage the fragile connection between Henry and Trip. Jordie will do anything to convince Henry to return, even playing on his prejudices and hinting at Trip's infidelity. But when the bank keeps calling with alerts on Henry's accounts, he suspects there's more going on with Jordie than a simple comeback music tour. Ultimately, Henry must choose where his heart lies, and who to trust, before he loses more than his chance at love.

iTunes

SNEAK PEEK

And now for a sneak peek of Book One in the Lowells of Honeywell, Texas, Untying His Not. If you'd like to preorder, follow this link.

June

"You're such a fucking joke, Lowell. You and your crippled brother."

Brock let the whiskey slide down his throat, wondering who he should swing at first. The big, stupid, quiet guy or the mouthy little shit at his side. They both worked the Crook-NeckCreek Ranch, so they were both equally appealing.

A voice of reason cautioned him that this could turn out badly, so he stayed where he was.

"I hear he found someone to marry him. Woman must be fugly as all get out. Is that why you been slappin' paint on that hellhole you call a ranch?"

Brock set his glass down very carefully on the bar, then turned to face the two men. The little guy it was.

With a mighty grunt, he drove his fist into Ronnie Critman's smug face. It was a bit of a reach because Ronnie had positioned himself just behind Beau Green's massive right arm in the hopes that Beau would take the brunt of whatever was dished out. At least, that was how their little game usually went.

This time, though, Ronnie must have been feeling too smug. Brock's fist landed perfectly, Ronnie's nasal bone collapsing with a satisfying, nauseating crunch. Ronnie went down immediately, and Beau looked on, obviously shocked. Brock grinned and staggered, trying to catch his balance. It didn't happen though. He was too toasted. As soon as he steadied, Beau got him. With a pile driver punch, Beau popped him twice in quick succession. Both lips split, then he got a fist to the temple, sending him into horrendous pain. But it was pain he'd felt before, so, manageable. Rocking back on his heels he tried to focus his double vision, lifting his fists. But it was too little, too late. Beau drove a fist into his ribs, stealing his wind, then swung wide to catch his jaw from beneath. His head snapped back painfully. Brock went down like a ton of bricks, his vision going dark.

When they got the call for the bar fight at Spur's mere minutes before her shift ended, Payton wasn't surprised. It was a Friday night and there wasn't that much to do in Honeywell, Texas other than hang out with your buddies and retell the same old stories. When you added liquor, though, it always made things more interesting. And it was Murphy's law that things had to happen just when you didn't want them to.

Dropping her iPad into her bag, she straightened in her seat as Charlie jerked to attention. They'd been hanging out in the parking lot of the new Sonic, sipping on milkshakes while they waited for the next call. Now, Charlie started the ambulance and pulled out carefully. When he reached the street, he flipped on the lights and siren and accelerated the big, boxy machine. Spur's was on the other side of town and out about six miles. If they pushed it they could be there in about ten minutes. Payton keyed the mic to let Donna know they were on their way, then tuned into the police channel.

Floyd County, Texas Sheriff's Department boasted twelve employees— a sheriff, five deputies, three radio operators and two detectives. There was normally another road deputy, but she was on maternity leave at the moment. So, they were a little short staffed. Payton heard three voices on the airwaves, though, and wondered what the hell they were getting into. It sounded like the entire department was at Spur's.

Then she heard Beau Green's name. Ah, no wonder they needed so many people to control the situation.

As they neared their destination her heartbeat picked up. This was the exciting part of the job. The challenging part was yet to come.

Charlie turned off the siren as they pulled into the lot. There were three police SUVs at the front of the bar, blue lights flashing. The sheriff's big tan truck was there as well. Beau Green leaned up against the hood of one vehicle, blood dripping from a cut on his forehead. There were two cops leaning against his back as they patted him down. Judging by the scowling, belligerent look on his face, it hadn't been an easy takedown. Payton had seen the look before.

In school he'd been the stereotypical bully, stealing money so that he could have more to eat at lunch. What Payton hadn't realized until years later was that he'd had no money to begin with. His mom had never given him any. Yes, he'd been a bully, but he'd been stealing so he could eat. School was the only real food he ever got.

In junior high she'd been too young to understand how rough he'd had it.

Beau had never given up his bully ways though.

And neither had Ronnie, who was currently sitting on a concrete parking curb wailing at the world. He was flailing his arms around and generally being a nuisance, demanding care.

Same old, same old.

As she hustled out of the rig, grabbing her bag on the way to the ground, she wondered who the two dickheads had roughed up. That was what they were known for doing, trying to get it over on other people, then acting like they hadn't done anything wrong.

The sheriff saw her and waved her toward him. When she drew close he guided her toward the front door of the bar.

"Just one patient. He hasn't come around after Beau clocked him."

Payton groaned internally. Yeah, that was understandable. Beau's hands were the size of milk jugs.

Surprisingly, the lights were on inside the bar. Payton wrinkled her nose as she looked around and realized how gross it was in the light. She ate here sometimes. Ew!

The sheriff led her around the edge of the long bar and waved to the floor. Payton saw a man lying there, unmoving, booted toes pointed skyward.

She drew close and dropped to her knees. It was only when she leaned over the patient when she realized who it was. Her stomach clutched in fear.

Brock Lowell.

Damn.

To anyone looking on, they would not have noticed the

slight hesitation when she realized who it was needing her care. They wouldn't realize how badly her heart shuddered when she saw him.

Payton dragged in a breath and started with the basics. Airway, breathing, circulation. There was a dripping cut on his forehead, and both of his lips were split on the left side. She leaned over to shine the penlight into his eyes. The brilliantly colored Caribbean blue-green iris of his right eye contracted perfectly, and so did the left. Well, that was good. Made his chance of serious concussion a little less. The loss of consciousness was concerning, though.

For a breathless beat of time, she suddenly realized how close she was to his mouth. It wouldn't normally be that big of a deal, but she knew how well that mouth could make a woman forget the world.

Clenching her jaw, she moved on down his body, looking for other injuries. Hands shaking, she reached out to undo the buttons down his chest. The further down she went the more her hands fumbled. Damn it. She shouldn't be reacting like this. Brock Lowell was an oblivious ass. He'd proven that time and time again. But for some reason he was her personal Kryptonite.

When she parted the halves of his shirt, she was dismayed to see a purpling bruise on his left rib area. Beau was right handed, so it made sense that most of Brock's damage was on that side. She palpated the injury, but he didn't move. There were no obvious breaks in the skin. She listened to his breathing. There was a bit of a rattle but more like a normal snore.

She poked him in the shoulder, wondering why he was unconscious. "Brock. Wake up!"

Thickly lashed lids opened and he stared up, seemingly dazed. Then he stretched his arms above his head and yawned. Mid-yawn he realized he was hurt and winced, curling in on himself.

"Oh, damn. What the hell?"

Payton scowled down at him. Had he seriously just been sleeping? "How do you feel?" she snapped.

He rolled his head and blinked up at her. "Oh, hey, Payton. What are you doing here, sweetness?"

A little shocked at the endearment, she wondered if he realized what he'd even said. She lifted her brows and looked around pointedly. "Uh, I'm cleaning your ass up off the floor. What are you doing here?"

Brock lifted his head three inches, did a swivel and dropped back to the ground. "This looks like Spur's."

"It is Spur's," she confirmed. "And you just had the crap beaten out of you. Do you remember that?"

He lifted a broad hand to rub at his face. "Yeah," he sighed. "It's coming back to me."

Payton refused to respond to the despondency she heard in his voice. He had made his bed. He could lie in it. "You received a heck of a knock on the head, and you might have a couple of broken ribs. I'll talk to Charlie and we'll run you into the hospital to get checked out."

Brock snorted and curled up into a sitting position. "Yeah, that's not happening. I'm fine."

She watched him try not to react to the pain in his side, but she'd been doing this job long enough that she could see through men and their stubbornness. He winced and his breath hitched in his broad chest. His face went ash white. But he forced his body straight. Then, with a Herculean effort, he climbed to his feet.

Brock swayed on his boot heels. Payton reached out to steady him but he shifted away from her touch to grab the heavy oak bar. "I'm good. Just got the wind knocked out of me."

Sheriff Lane moved close enough to grab Brock as well. Payton moved aside to let the big man closer. The Sheriff had only been on the job about five years, but he had a good head on his massive shoulders.

"You need to listen to Payton, Brock. I don't think it would hurt to get checked out."

Brock shook his dark head and swung down to grab his black Stetson from the floor. His arms went pinwheeling, but he still managed to keep his feet as he jammed the hat over his black curls. "I'm good, damn it. She just wants to get her damn hands on me."

Payton felt the blush creep into her cheeks and it pissed her off more than anything that he could still get a rise out of her. "You're a hard-headed goat, Brock Lowell, but it's my job to make sure you're okay, whether you want me to or not."

"Whatever."

"So, are you refusing care?"

"Hell, yes, I'm refusing care."

Sheriff Lane held up a hand to stop Brock from walking away.

"You need to chill out a little bit, Brock. She's trying to help you."

Brock snorted and headed out the door of the bar. As soon as he saw Ronnie, who was now in handcuffs, he smirked. "When you gonna learn to keep your mouth shut, Critman?"

Sheriff Lane grasped his arm. "Back of my truck, Lowell. You're in no shape to be left alone."

Brock jerked his arm away in anger, and Payton winced. He was only making it worse for himself.

"Why are you taking me to jail? They started it."

Sheriff shook his head. "I know they're mouthy, but I have witness statements that you took the first swing. You either go with me peacefully or I charge you. Which is it?"

Brock scowled. "You're just Mr. Goody-two-shoes, aren't you Sheridan? You won't arrest me because it'll make my sister mad."

The sheriff laughed and shook his head. "I think your sister would tell me to haul you to jail and throw away the key."

Payton snorted as well, because that's exactly what would happen. Cheyenne Lowell pulled no punches and had no patience for stupidity. There were too many other things going on that needed their attention.

And he knew that, even as drunk as he was. With a wince, Brock headed in the direction the sheriff pointed and climbed into the back of the SUV. Payton caught the gasp as he climbed in and pulled the door shut behind himself.

Payton and the sheriff shared a look. "If he starts to throw up or anything," she warned, "let me know. I think he just passed out on the floor in there. Beau's fist helped him down, and he'll be sore tomorrow, but I think he'll be okay."

Sheriff Lane nodded. "Yeah. I thought he was done working out his issues."

Payton sighed. "I know, Sheridan. I think Chad's wedding news has him extra shook."

The sheriff turned to her, head cocked. "Wait, Chad's getting married?"

Payton nodded. "I talked to Cheyenne earlier. It's not going to be a big affair, but they want to have it on the ranch in a few months. You hadn't heard?"

Sheridan shook his head. "Nah, I was in a conference in Austin till a few hours ago."

Sighing, she reached out to rest a hand on her friend's arm, then turned to head back to the rig. She was a little younger than Chad, but they'd been in high school together. She remembered all the excitement when he left for the Marines, then the following heartbreak when he came back wounded. Lora seemed to be the perfect match for him, and he'd waited patiently for her to be ready for marriage.

Seems like everyone else around here was striking out.

She glanced at the sheriff's truck again. Brock had tipped his head back against the seat and his eyes were shut. For a moment, just before Sheridan pulled away, Brock lifted his head and opened his eyes. Payton waited for him to turn his head and look at her, but he didn't.

Well, wasn't that the story of her life?

Brock's story, Untying his Not, will be available at the end of August on all platforms. You can preorder now!